Hello Santa

A Christmas Story

ETHAN FALLS

Copyright © 2023 by Ethan Falls.

All rights reserved. No part of this book may be reproduced in any form or by any electronic or mechanical means, including information storage and retrieval systems, without permission in writing from the publisher, except by reviewers, who may quote brief passages in a review.

This publication contains the opinions and ideas of its author. It is intended to provide helpful and informative material on the subjects addressed in the publication. The author and publisher specifically disclaim all responsibility for any liability, loss, or risk, personal or otherwise, which is incurred as a consequence, directly or indirectly, of the use and application of any of the contents of this book.

WRITERS REPUBLIC L.L.C.
515 Summit Ave. Unit R1
Union City, NJ 07087, USA

Website: *www.writersrepublic.com*
Hotline: *1-877-656-6838*
Email: *info@writersrepublic.com*

Ordering Information:
Quantity sales. Special discounts are available on quantity purchases by corporations, associations, and others. For details, contact the publisher at the address above.

Library of Congress Control Number:	2023918248
ISBN-13: 979-8-89100-237-1	[Paperback Edition]
979-8-89100-238-8	[Hardback Edition]
979-8-89100-236-4	[Digital Edition]

Rev. date: 09/18/2023

Disclaimer

Only if you are nine years of age or older will you be able to understand the complexities of this story.

Chapter

1

First summer transitioned to fall, and then fall transitioned to winter. Soon the snow began to fall, and the children of the neighborhood began their winter festivities.

As Christmas approached and Thanksgiving became a gobbled memory, lights began to illuminate the fronts of homes, and carols of joy rang throughout homes filled with dreams of Santa.

When the sun came up and sparkles of light began to glimmer off the snow that had settled on the ground overnight, children began to emerge from their homes with a desire of creating figures of winter cheer from the new layers of bright white snow.

At the end of the day, sticks poked into rounded bodies would continue to wave to passersby, even as the children who were all at play made their way back home for the night.

As he emerged from the back door to the small porch with four steps that were covered in a new layer of thick white snowball supply, Johnny Ingersol stopped and took in the beautiful white landscape that he was eager to trample through on his way to wherever it was that he wanted to go. But he hated walking. Especially through a lot of snow.

As he stood gandering his first play excursion, Johnny looked over and saw his bike that had ridden with him through the whole summer. It sat looking lonely as it gripped the garage wall, as it had been doing, for several months. It was covered in a tall layer of snow, and the bike's chain was covered in a layer of orange rust.

The bike's chain was the only part of the bike that wasn't invisible because of the bike's white frame. Johnny missed getting on the bike's fat seat and shoving the pedals forward as he gathered speed as quickly as he could and tried to ride around the block faster than anyone had ever ridden around his block before.

He was as fast as lightning; and not even Josephine, who lived several houses down, could ever ride around the block as fast as him.

Johnny walked down the four steps of the porch, careful not to let his boots slide off the lip of the stair. He had fallen down the snow-covered stairs before, and he was careful never to do it again.

When he got to the bottom of the stairs, he began plowing through the snow to where his bike stood against the garage. When he got to where his bike stood in the snow, he reached out and yanked the bike by the handlebars and knocked the snow off it with his gloved hand.

He had never ridden his bike in the snow before, and he was shocked that he had never thought of it. He pulled the bike through the thick snow to where the outline of the driveway began.

He rooted the bike on the snow-covered pavement of the driveway and pulled his snowsuit pants legs up so he could throw his leg over the bike's frame. He threw one leg over the bike and rearranged his snowsuit so it wasn't up his crack as he sat on the bike's seat.

He balanced himself and put both feet on the pedals and began propelling himself forward, but as he began moving forward, both of his boots slipped off both of the pedals, and the bike began to slide sideways.

With a sideways glance, Johnny saw the ground coming straight at him. He braced himself for the impact, and his fall seemed to last forever. It was at that moment, as he waited for the pain from his fall to arrive, that he realized why he never saw kids riding through the neighborhood on their bikes in the winter. In the snow, kids were bad drivers.

Winter was the best time of the year for Johnny Ingersol. He could get the kids good in the winter, especially at the playground where the kids were abundant, and there were good times to be had by all. Johnny liked to pick on kids, and the more kids there were, the more fun he could have.

Hello Santa

Johnny Ingersol that's his name, "And don't forget it!" That's what he said to kids on the playground after he pushed them down to the ground. Most often, they would fall flat on their butts, and boy, did it hurt when their tailbones hit the ground, or the ice if they were playing down by the frozen creek.

Being one of those kids that could empty a playground always gave Johnny a sense of accomplishment. But in the winter, it could be tough. Nobody ever wanted to come out and play with him, and when they did come out to play, they almost always went home early.

If they were sledding on the hill, after he pushed them down the hill so hard that they ended up in the creek, they would have to go home because they would be soaked from creek water. But someone always got ice-water bitten when Johnny was sledding on Gobbler's Hill.

He especially liked pushing Martha down the hill extra fast toward the creek; and most days she went home wet, mad, and cursing at Johnny.

"You're an angel killer, Johnny Ingersol!" Martha would scream at him from the bottom of the hill after she got cold-water bitten by Johnny and the creek.

If it wasn't getting other kids soaked in the creek that made kids not want to play with him, then it was the playground where he was always on the lookout for any wedgie victims. Little tufts of underwear peering out of a boy's jeans were always a good time to move in like a cheetah on the prowl and start a yanking hard enough to chaff any crack. But that wasn't so easy when all the kids wore snowsuits.

During the winter months, unless it was too cold to play outside, the list of good things to do was long; and Johnny could keep himself busy out of the house so he wouldn't have to go home and do chores.

Every time he went home, his mom would start telling him to do stuff, but his idea of doing stuff around the house was playing outside all around it. If he had to, he would even stand and make yellow words in the snow so he wouldn't have to go home and take out the trash.

In the winter, there are a lot of good things to do like sledding, building igloos, snowball fights, and, Johnny's favorite of all, talking kids into putting their tongues on cold metal fence posts.

"It's not cold enough for your tongue to stick to it, you dummy!" Johnny would proclaim to the doubting children of his cold-weather knowledge.

"It has to be so cold out that your nipples turn blue!" That's what he always said to the other kids to get them to understand.

Johnny would tell them, "It's physics, silly! I read that it's all about hot and cold. When it gets really cold out, your nipples turn blue because they get cold. You should know that!"

The kids stood standing and staring at him, not understanding anything that he was talking about. The confused look on their faces only grew as Johnny blabbered on and on about his Eskimo knowledge of the winter.

"Your nipples weren't blue this morning when you got dressed, were they?" Johnny would begin to wave at the fence post with both hands, welcoming them to touch it with the tip of their tongue as he spoke.

Once in a while, he would catch one of the kids in the neighborhood off guard, but not too often did he get a squirmer at the fence post. That's what he called anyone that got stuck to the post with their tongue. A squirmer.

Since the weather had started getting colder, he had yet to get an opportunity with any of the other kids to get them to put their tongue to the fence post. When Johnny did get an opportunity to try it on someone, he wouldn't waste any time.

One thing that all the kids learned pretty quickly about Johnny Ingersol was that he never wasted an opportunity.

One day Josephine was walking by as he was yelling at a group of boys and pointing to a metal post. He watched her as she stopped and watched them. She was trying to understand what they were talking about, but she was too far away to hear what they were saying.

He was trying to convince them about something. That she figured out. But the boys walked away before she could cross the street to find out what they were saying.

Josephine loved to get the goods on other kids so she would have something to tease them about. So if there was something she could find out about a kid, she wanted to know.

She loved teasing kids, and gossip was her favorite. But as soon as she got over to where he was standing, Johnny started trying to convince her. She never believed anything that Johnny ever said, and when he started trying to convince her more and more, she started getting mad at him.

"Every time you open your word hole, the lying ones always come out, Johnny Ingersol!" Josephine said to him as she poked him in his chest repeatedly. But Josephine was caught unsuspectingly by Johnny, and being a know-it-all herself, she couldn't stand to hear Johnny say another word about the fence post.

"It's because you're a girl that you don't believe me." Johnny scowled at her.

And that was all it took to get Josephine going.

She hardly ever listened to Johnny because he was like a blubbering whale on ice skates, constantly jabbering and moving his lips all over. He must have done three circles around the fence post waiting for her to answer him, but she just watched him as he waved his arms back and forth like he was a mime.

"You just don't believe me because you know I'm always right!" Johnny said to her as he looked down menacingly at the fence post and then slowly back to her.

She glared back at him and then stared over at the post as if it were a third party to the conversation. She looked at it and waited as Johnny stared at her.

But while he waited for a reply, she didn't answer him. She just stood and stared at him with a dirty look on her face, and she wanted to prove him wrong. Instead of answering him, she stuck her tongue out and put the tip of it to the fence post. The first thought that came to her mind as her tongue began to stick to the post was, *My nipples weren't blue!*

She was mad as all get out and her face started to turn red with anger. Not just because her tongue was stuck, but because she was wrong.

"You turd face!" she tried getting out with no tongue to help her make the words. Again and again, she pulled on her tongue as the tip of it clung to the post as the rest of her tongue grew skinnier and skinnier as she tried to tug it free.

But there Josephine stood, with her tongue stuck where she knew it didn't belong, yelling at Johnny with words that he could barely understand.

"Ladies and gentlemen, we have a squirmer!" Johnny shouted as he walked away, leaving her throwing her fist up and yelling at him.

"Turd face!" he heard Josephine yelling over and over again as the sound of her got quieter and quieter as he walked further and further away.

I will get him one day, Josephine thought as she watched him walking down the street laughing and swinging his arms and butt back and forth.

He looked back at her several times to see if she was still squirming, and sure enough, she continued to raise her fist at him and yelled and tugged at her tongue, which stayed stuck. The big grin on his face seemed to get larger every time he looked back.

Later that day, upon Johnny's arrival at the playground, the joyful calls of kids at play would stir his mind and get him thinking, *Hmm, who will be first on my list?* After he scans the faces to see who has smiles and who doesn't, he picks Josephine. But then he thinks better of it.

Maybe Timmy could be my next victim, Johnny thought. Perhaps he could send a snowball right into the chompers of an unsuspecting pirate standing on the playground ship, sliding back and forth as he shook the ship's wheel.

Johnny watched from a park bench as all the kids ran back and forth, their snowsuits sometimes tangling up their feet and sending them sprawling forward, but all of them were immune to the pain with the excitement of good play.

"Batten down the hatches!" a boy screamed out as several other boys bustled around him trying to save the ship. They began sliding on ice-covered floors that were acting as gangplanks and attempting to send them all overboard.

At nine years old, most of the time it is deciding what it is that you want to play first, and sometimes the decision isn't always easy to make because there can be so many fun things to do.

Sometimes there are so many decisions that are not always easy. Should I make a snowman, or should I go sledding? But Johnny was not that kind of kid though. Johnny knew exactly what it was he wanted to do every day, and what he wanted to do every day more than anything else was to pick on other kids.

He liked doing things like walking up to other kids who were playing in the snow, especially Martha, doing things like making snow angels in the virgin snow.

Johnny would watch from afar as the girls would lie down in the snow and wave their arms and legs back and forth and scream out in song the "Revenge of the Snowman" lyrics.

"How dare you make me melt, Mister Heater Man!" the girls sang as their arms and legs flailed back and forth, spreading the snow into clustered piles.

"But thank you for giving me a puddle to play in!" one of the girls began to sing.

It is probably Josephine, he thought. *She always calls herself a singer and a star!*

Johnny would just stand and watch them and cover his ears until they were all done trying to make him throw up with all their singing and joyful laughter.

I will give them something to laugh about, he thought as he waited for them to finish.

As the girls got up and looked down to admire their works of creativity, that's when Johnny would walk over and kick his way through the snow as he walked in front of them. He would laugh as his feet trampled their snow angels as they looked on in horror.

"Johnny, you're an angel killer!" Martha yelled out at him one day when he went to work on her masterpiece.

The snow angel looked up at her from the ground begging her to make him stop.

Martha looked at him with an angry face and spoke with a bitter tone in her voice as she promised to get him during Christmas vacation.

Making fun of other kids was high on Johnny's to-do list because it was so much fun. Johnny would say, "How could I not make fun of a kid who got bird poop all over his face on his way to school?"

"Hey, poopface?" Johnny called out to Timmy that day in the hall.

Timmy got to school, and Johnny saw the white poop all over his face and shirt, and he exploded with laughter.

All day he tried and tried to get Timmy to cry by teasing him, but Timmy just threatened to put up his dukes all day long. Johnny knew that Timmy couldn't fight his way out of a smoke cloud, so he gave up in frustration.

Johnny knew that if he couldn't get the kids at school to cry, then spitballs were another great way to have some fun. But if that didn't work, then it was his wet finger in a kid's ear that would be fun too. If he couldn't make them cry, then grossing kids out worked too, if he wanted to have some fun.

Johnny liked talking and making fun of kids, and he even liked to tell kids things even if he wasn't sure if they were true or not.

"If someone says it's true, then it has to be true." That was what the guy at the carnival stand told him last summer every time he went with the other kids to play the games to win prizes.

Johnny especially liked winning the monster-faced erasers he could stick on the end of his pencil. He knew that the guys that run the games at the carnival were really smart because Josephine agrees with him, and she never agrees with him about anything.

"Your mom sleeps with the mailman!" Johnny told a kid on the playground one day, and he expected the boy to get mad at him. He liked to get other kids mad. They would never fight him though, but he did wish that just once a kid would put up his dukes.

"Who's the mailman?" was the reply from one of the boys, but the insult went over the boy's head like a helium balloon.

"You're going to get warts because you touched a frog!" Johnny told a girl on the playground, sending her home reeling from the trauma of the thought of having warts all over her body tomorrow, even on her eyeball lids.

"They will get all over your eyeball lids, and you will only be able to see through a crack!" he told her. He laughed as she ran all the way home, tears falling down her cheek as she looked back at him as she ran.

But Johnny's ultimate favorite was sharing his lunch with the kids. If they weren't willing to play with him because he was being mean, then Johnny would go home and have lunch and come back to the playground.

Sometimes all the playing and running around would get his stomach upset, and most of the kids knew to watch out for him after lunch if they were smart.

"It couldn't be the twelve cupcakes you had for lunch that made you sick, could it?" That was what Johnny's mom said to him after he ran home one day and told her that he accidentally barfed all over Timmy.

Chapter 2

When Martha dreamed, she dreamed big. She dreamed of starships and planets and everything else that was big. She liked to look up into the sky at night and imagine everything that was up there.

"Martha Morris extraordinaire!" she would proclaim.

Her dreams were big, but she felt she couldn't decide. She wasn't sure what she wanted to be when she grew up, and she was tired of her mother asking her. Every morning at breakfast, her mother would ask her the same question.

"What do you want to be when you grow up, Martha?" is how her mother often started the breakfast talk.

She thought that she might want to be a person who fixes people like a doctor. But she also might want to be a lawyer because her mom says that they make a lot of money because they can lie well. But she doesn't think that she wants to tell lies to people to make money. That just seemed too easy of a job for her. She would much rather do something she liked.

She also thought that she could be a garbage man when she grew up because she could get anything she wanted for free. People always throw away a lot of things that she couldn't imagine people would want to get rid of.

Martha has seen all kinds of things people put out on the road for the garbage man to collect, and some lucky people even get to drive around and get all kinds of stuff for free. Her mom doesn't have money to buy stuff, so what better way to get the things she needs than for free?

Martha's problem though was that she could never decide.

Sometimes deciding is even worse than figuring things out, she thought.

Decisions were big, and she knew it, but she also knew that if she didn't make the right decisions, then the rest of her life would be ruined. Her mom always tells her that she has to be smart and make good decisions if she is going to be successful.

Ooh, the pressures of a kid, Martha thought.

Martha just wanted to sit and play with her dolls all day long if her mother would ever let her. She just wanted to play with them forever. She knew that when she grew up, she was still going to play with her dolls.

She was even going to take them to work with her, and if they didn't let her take her dolls to work with her, then she was going to quit her job. It was either that or wait patiently all year for take-your-doll-to-work day. *If they have one of those*, she thought.

She could play with her dolls all day long, and it was the things they could do that made her want to play with them so much. She could make them do anything she wanted them to do, and she loved to make them do things. She liked to make them have tea with her, and the parties that she had with her dolls were always the best parties in the neighborhood.

Miss Molly is her favorite doll, but Miss Molly doesn't like to drink tea, and that is unfortunate because Martha loves to have tea parties. Miss Barb used to be her favorite doll because they loved having tea parties together, but Miss Barb had a very tragic end to what was a wonderful day until Josephine wanted to play.

She and Miss Barb would get all dressed up, and Miss Barb would pour them both a cup of tea, and they would discuss important things like the weather and how not to be the dumbest kid in school.

For hours the two of them would sit and drink tea and talk about all the wonderful things they could do together. One day, Josephine came over to play, and the two of them were having a lot of fun until Josephine ripped Miss Barb's arm off. Now Miss Barb just sits there because Martha doesn't like one-arm dolls anymore.

So now, she and Miss Molly, who is now her new favorite doll, will sit and pretend they are reading the newspaper together because Miss Molly likes reading the newspaper. The two of them will sit and read the paper or will get dressed up and have pity parties. Martha overheard her mom saying that a lot of people have those, and Miss Molly loves them too.

When she and Miss Barb played together, Martha never had to wash the teacups because Miss Barb always did the dishes. For that, Martha was grateful because Miss Molly never does any of the dishes, especially after they had wonderful pity parties together.

So now the dishes are all stacked up because Miss Barb only has one arm and can't do them anymore.

Miss Molly doesn't like doing dishes, so now she has to do them all, and she doesn't like washing dishes.

"Martha?" her mother yelled up to her as she was looking at the pile of teacups in her plastic kitchen sink. She so wishes Miss Barb could do the dishes for her.

"Martha, tomorrow is a snow day. You can stay up until ten!" she finished yelling up the stairs to her from the bottom of the landing.

Martha was so excited she grabbed Miss Molly out of her chair and started talking to her.

"Miss Molly, I don't have school tomorrow, so we can play all day together," she said to the doll as she picked up a brush and started brushing the doll's hair.

"Miss Molly, we are going to get dressed up fancy tonight, and then we are going to go to a pity party." Martha petted the doll's hair softly and looked into the doll's gleaming green eyes.

"And tonight, when we are at the party, we are going to have all the humble pie we can eat! Mom says it's good for people. And we need to take care of you, Miss Molly, so you're big and strong and don't get your arm ripped off!"

Martha loved winter, and she liked it when they got to have a snow day. It could have been her favorite day of the year, but when she got to go see Santa—that might be her favorite day of the year.

She is so excited to have the whole day to just sit and play with her dolls, but she does miss the summer though. If she could have half of her summer during the winter, she would be even more happy.

During the summer, she always got to spend all day at the playground, and she liked the playground very much. It was her favorite time of play.

Timmy was always playing on the pirate ship, where all the kids liked chasing each other around with imaginary swords. They would pretend a fatal thrust, and then another kid would slowly fall to the ground, putting his dying breath on display for all to admire.

Sometimes Martha would sit and draw in the sand, pictures of her dolls driving through the desert on their way to a vacation in the sun.

She liked to stay at the playground all day, and if she needed something to drink, she would always grab Timmy's juice and drink it. Timmy always carried a bottle with juice in it everywhere he went, and it was really handy if she ever needed a drink.

"Why go home?" she would ask herself.

One day, while Timmy was busy getting all the other pirates to board another ship, she went over under the pirate ship. And tucked away in the corner where nobody could see was Timmy's bottle with lazily cold juice sitting inside of it calling for her to come and take a drink. Martha was dying of thirst because the sun had warmed her ever so much, and the thought of his cold juice, how could she ever resist!

To Martha's horror, Timmy had put ink on the rim of his bottle to discover who was drinking his juice at the playground. Timmy hated people who drank his juice and was worried he would get lip-fall-off syndrome if he touched someone's lips.

Martha didn't know that he had put ink on the mouth of the bottle, and when she put her mouth in the opening of his juice, she got ink in the form of a circle around her lips.

For two weeks at the playground, she had a circle around her lips. Each day it would get lighter and lighter, but for Timmy, the sight of that circle stayed there forever.

"Timmy!" Martha said as she knocked on his front door. "Timmy!" she said as she knocked again.

"Hi, Martha!" Timmy said with a smile and a polite wave as he opened the front door to greet her.

As he opened the screen door and looked down at her, the crescent-shaped imprint of the ink stood out above and below her lips but was getting fainter and harder to see.

But she didn't just take a drink from his bottle, she drank the whole thing! Maybe that's why the ink stayed for so long, Timmy thought.

"Timmy, let me use your bathroom. I have to poop, and I won't be able to make it home!"

She stood staring up at him, both fists clenching her stomach as if trying to grab the pain.

"I punched my cheeks together, but it's going to fly out!" Martha said with urgency in her tone.

He saw the seriousness in her eyes, and he was very aware of how bad it can be when there is no warning and you have to go. Timmy pulled the door open wide so she could run past him to get to the bathroom.

Martha ran up the front steps and shot past him and ran to the bathroom, but as the door closed behind her, a slam rang out that echoed throughout the house.

"Timmy? Is that you, Timmy? Please go upstairs and clean your room and stay inside this house until it is clean enough to show off to the Queen of Sibley!" his mother said from the kitchen.

Timmy was so mad. He looked at the bathroom door that Martha had locked behind her. Martha let his mom know that he was home, and now he was going to be stuck smelling his socks as he cleaned his room for an hour.

The last ten times he had been told to clean his room, he just shoved everything under the bed until his mom came up and told him he did a wonderful job cleaning his room. Then he pulled the mess back out from underneath it, and he had his dirty room back.

Martha sat down on the toilet in the bathroom and listened to hear if anyone was near the door, but it was quiet. Then she heard Timmy as he made his way up the stairs after getting yelled at by his mother, but otherwise, it was silent.

She sat on the toilet for a couple of minutes, but she didn't have to go to the bathroom.

She stood up after she thought it would be long enough and pulled a little pouch out of her pants pocket. She pulled the toilet lid up and sprinkled the itching powder on the toilet seat and put the pouch back into her pants pocket.

She put the toilet lid back down and flushed the toilet twice just so he knew that she was doing real business and that's why it took two flushes.

After she was done, she opened the bathroom door and ran for the front door.

"Thank you, Timmy! Thank you, Timmy's mom!" she yelled even louder as she ran for the front door so she could make her way back over to the playground.

An hour later, Timmy came up to the playground with his juice bottle in his hand, but she had no interest in drinking anything he brought over to the playground ever again. Timmy took his usual spot up on the pirate ship, at the helm.

Martha sat and drew in the sand, and every time she looked over at the pirate ship, Timmy's hand was digging down into the back of his pants and itching away at his butt crack.

Chapter 3

"Timmy, you should never use the word *hate*. It's unbecoming of you, and you're better than that!"

That's what his mom always said every time he used the most reasonable way to describe getting picked on. He hated getting picked on. Especially by Johnny. He didn't mind when Josephine picked on him because he knew that she was so full of hot air that if she blew up a balloon it would float away—high into the sky.

But when an old man that was sitting in a restaurant running his teeth across bony barbecue ribs could use your arms for a toothpick when he was done, then you weren't going to be standing up against a bully. Or a little sister for that matter, and sometimes his little sister even scared him half out of his wits.

Timmy's little sister always tried to scare him, and he hated it. She jumped out of a garbage can that was in the garage one day, and he was so scared that he peed his pants. He had to let it go because if he held it in, it would come out of his ears.

"If you got frightened and held your pee in, then it would find another way to get out. Like your ears," Martha told him one day as they were playing on the playground.

She always helped him with his homework, and she was really smart, and he believed her. When she told him that, he knew that if he ever got that scared, he would just pee his pants because he didn't want anyone to see pee coming out of his ears.

For Timmy, it was just a day in the life of being the smartest kid in school. He knew that he had to listen to people if he was ever going to learn anything. Martha taught him a lot, but Miss Beaker was a big help too—that is, unless you made her mad. Then Miss Beaker yelled at the kids, and she wasn't teaching them anything while she was busy yelling at them.

He liked being able to raise his hand in class before anyone else to answer one of her questions. Martha sat a couple of seats over from him, and she tried to raise her hand first all the time against him, and he hated it.

Martha isn't the smartest girl in school though he didn't think. So sometimes he would let her raise her hand first just because he didn't want to. After all, his arm got tired from holding it up while Miss Beaker looked across the room at the children deciding which one of them it was that she would want to hear speak. He was sure of it because he could tell anyone's thoughts just by the look on their face.

When Timmy looked around at the boys in his class, he thought he knew who was the smartest and who was the dumbest kid in the class. He was, of course, the smartest boy in class; and most of the time, the dumbest boy is the one causing trouble and leaving tacks on your chair when you get up to throw something in the garbage can or to sharpen your pencil.

It was Johnny that did it most of the time. Trying to hold in the exasperation of having to pull a sharp pointy object out of a defenseless butt cheek can be a challenge for sure. Timmy's problem was that it was always his hand on the seat before his crack, so a tack in the palm of his hand always got him going. A laugh from Johnny sitting behind him always made him even madder.

"You stop that right now!" Miss Beaker blared at him as he shook his hand back and forth to try and get the tack out of it.

He hated Johnny.

One day at the playground when everybody was having fun, Timmy took a pen that he found on the playground and pulled the plastic tube out of the pen and pulled the head off. He put the clean end to his mouth and blew out the ink from the pen tube onto Johnny's seat of his bicycle.

Johnny always had his bicycle at the playground, and now and then Timmy would let the air out of his tires to get even with him when he pushed him down or barfed on him.

That day when Johnny left the playground, the ink that Timmy put on his seat got all over his pants, and for weeks after that day, Johnny's skin would be stained with ink. Timmy could only laugh in silence, but he was pretty sure that Johnny knew it was him that put the ink on his seat.

When Johnny got done riding his bike home that day, his mom asked him, "What did you do to your pants? They were brand-new! You know I'm not made of money!"

Johnny looked down, and there it was. A huge stain of blue ink was all over the crotch of his pants. Johnny was furious at Timmy. He knew it was him, but he wasn't completely sure. He tried every day after school to get Timmy to put up his dukes, but all Timmy would do is laugh at him and call him Blue Balls.

Johnny would never forget the day Timmy made his balls turn blue though. For a month after that day, every time he took a bath, he would look down into his bath water and declare, "Save the Smurf!"

One day Johnny asked his mom, "Mom, can I have a pickle with my lunch?"

His mother was more than happy to make sure that he had a nice pickle with his sandwich and some cookies.

That whole morning Johnny couldn't get his mind off the green pickle that sat in his lunch box. Later that day, after lunch was over, Johnny took the pickle his mom put in his lunch out of the plastic bag and shoved it down the back of Timmy's pants into his crack as he was walking down the hall to class.

"Oh," Timmy howled as it began burning, all while he was trying to flush the pickle out of his butt crack. As it burned, Timmy ran to the office where the nurse quietly attempted to calm the burn out of his backside.

In class the next day, Johnny leaned over to Timmy who sat a couple of seats in front of him in class and whispered. "How's your butt crack, Timmy?"

"Shut up!" he yelled out at Johnny, and it was loud enough to get the teacher to turn her head and look to see what the fuss among the students was all about.

"Who was that?" Miss Beaker scowled as she turned around to look at the children all sitting up straight and scared of her wrath. Her aged face made her scowl look even meaner.

"It was Timmy!" Johnny said as he pointed at him, trying to hold back a good laugh that was just barely controllable.

"Timmy, come up to the front of the class and write twenty-five times on the board, 'I will not interrupt or speak out in the class.'"

Timmy was not happy when he had to go up to the front of the class with everybody looking at him, but he stomped to the blackboard and began writing out his sentences as all the other children stared at him as he wrote.

After lunch, and after Timmy had finished writing out all of his sentences, the kids all ushered their way back to class from the lunchroom.

Johnny didn't have time for lunch, and he didn't like the sloppy joe in the lunch line, so he skipped the meal line and snuck back to class.

When the bell rang, all the trays were neatly stacked, and all the kids made their way back to class.

Patiently, the children waited for the teacher, and as she stepped into the room, the kids all burst out laughing as they looked up at her. Miss Beaker didn't understand at first that it wasn't her that the children were laughing at. But when she looked behind her, she realized what had happened.

Where Timmy had written out his sentences on the blackboard, someone had erased part of the top sentence, which now read, "I will not flush pickles in the crack of my butt."

The teacher huffed and puffed, and Johnny thought for sure the top of her head was going to come off, but the smoke coming out of Timmy's ears could have filled the classroom.

"I have so much fun with the kids at school, Mom," Johnny told his mom that night at the dinner table.

Chapter 4

"Josephine, come down here and get your breakfast!" her mother yelled up at her.

She had sleepy eyes and had absolutely no interest in getting up. The crust that was in the corner of her eyes was keeping them from opening all the way, but she wasn't interested in opening them in the first place.

She lay still in bed, and then she remembered that she didn't have to get up for school today! Maybe the last day of school tomorrow will be a snow day too, and then she wouldn't have to go to school for the rest of the year!

That would be perfect! she thought as she tried opening her eyes, feeling the crust on her eyelids breaking apart.

She wished that she didn't have to go to school for the rest of her life. That would be even better. She could just lay in her bed and rest her eyeballs for as long as she wanted.

Martha told her that people that use their eyes a lot go blind when they get old. Martha is the smartest girl in school, and the carnival guys said that if someone says it's true, then it's true. Josephine doesn't like to believe Martha, but if it was true, she didn't want to wear out her eyeballs before she got old.

Josephine sat up in her bed and looked out the window. She watched as the snow came down in the form of huge flakes that seemed to stack one on top of another.

Ooh, what a day it was going to be, she thought as she sat on the edge of the bed.

The floor was cold on her bare feet, but she grabbed her blanket and wrapped it around herself as she sat and watched the small white figures float past her window.

It was not that often that she had to stay home from school because it was snowing, and she couldn't wait to get started doing whatever it was that she wanted to do.

The first thing she wanted to do on her snow day was to stay in bed and practice keeping her sheets warm. She lay back down on her bed and covered herself with her quilt and closed her eyes.

She loved the winter and loved playing in the snow, but when she was in her pajamas, it was very important to stay under the covers. They kept her nice and warm, and she didn't like being cold.

The second thing she was going to do on her snow day was to stay in bed and practice getting some more sleep. She will make her mother call her downstairs ten times, and if she wants to go downstairs and eat, she will. If she doesn't, she won't.

Josephine was constantly called stubborn and lazy by her mother, but she didn't believe it. It is not easy to stay in bed and be lazy all day. Josephine thought it was difficult to do nothing all day. If she didn't do anything all day, she would be bored, and she never felt bored. She just wanted options, and she knew that if you stayed in bed, then you had the option to sleep if she wanted to.

She didn't believe anything that anybody had to say, and it was especially true if her mother said she was lazy. As far as she knew, she was always right anyway. Even if she wasn't right, she would still insist to herself that she was.

On some days like today, if her lazy bones were acting up, she simply kept them from moving. Josephine was lazy, but today was a snow day, and there wasn't anything she was going to do if she didn't want to.

Chapter

5

"Josephine! Get down here!" her mother yelled up at her again.

"Ugh," Josephine murmured as she threw off her blankets and began stomping over to her bedroom door.

"So much for doing what I want to do!" Josephine yelled out her door and down the steps hoping that her mother would hear her. She slammed the door shut and walked to the window and watched the snow blowing around and piling up outside in drifts.

She got dressed and put all her treasures in her pockets. That's what she called them. She had three more gunpowder sticks, at least that's what she pretended them to be. When you threw them against something hard, they would explode and make a loud popping sound.

She had her piece of black chalk that she put in one pocket and a rabbit's foot and her four lucky pennies she put in the other. She figured you could take your one lucky penny and give it three friends. The lucky penny could rub off on them, and then you would have four times the luck!

She loved her rabbit's foot, and she loved rabbits too. She was glad that they were willing to give up their feet so people could have good luck. Though she always wondered how bunnies got around on stumps if they gave up their feet.

Down in the rabbit hole was where the rabbit's feet came from, she thought as she shoved the rabbit's foot deep down into her other pocket.

Josephine, against her will, made her way downstairs and to the kitchen and sat down, listening to her mother clean in the other room. She ate her breakfast and sat at the table while waiting for her orange juice to disappear into her tummy.

She looked at the glass of juice sitting on the table in front of her, but she was feeling too lazy and didn't want to reach her arm out to grab it.

Maybe she should tell her mom that she wants a robot for Christmas. That way she could make a robot do everything for her. She could plug it in when she got it home from the store and then start telling it what to do.

She liked telling things and people what to do. When she grows up, she wants to be the person that could tell anyone she talked to what to do. Maybe she could be president. She could go to anyone's house, and they would have to do what she said because she was the president.

"Josephine, take out the garbage, please!" she heard her mother shout out from in the other room.

She got a mad look on her face and folded her arms across her chest.

"Hmm, I didn't hear you, Mom!" she yelled back at her mother.

This day was not going the way she planned it when she had first woken up. She had it planned out perfectly. First, she was going to stay in bed, and then she was going to go play after she ate her breakfast, but she couldn't recall a single chore she put on her fun list for the day.

Josephine got up from the table and put her dish in the sink silently and tiptoed to the back door where her snowsuit and hat and gloves waited for her. She looked around the corner and saw her mom dusting in the living room, so very quietly she got all of her snow clothes on and grabbed her sled, and walked out the back door.

Josephine chugged her way through the thick pile of snow covering everything. The Christmas lights left on overnight were barely visible as the sun came out and the snowy storm clouds vanished over the horizon.

The trees and their bare, boney-like branches were coated with a layer of white fluff. Gentle breezes disturbed the snow on the branches above, and the fallen snow began to fall once more as the wind wafted it from its wooden perch.

Looking down the street toward the open land of fresh white snow, the breeze littered the air with sparkles as the sun gleamed through frozen flakes riding on the wind.

Down the street, Josephine left boot trails and a smooth indent from the weight of the sled as she pulled it along. She made her way to the hill that was down a few blocks at the end of the street. To her delight, there was nobody atop Gobbler's Hill.

It was the famous Gobbler's Hill where all the kids tested whether they were true sledders or not. It was for Josephine, on top of Gobbler's Hill, where all the kids in the neighborhood would gather throughout the day to test the snow and ride the white wave downward, which Josephine would attempt to sled down to the creek without falling in.

The creek water was always really cold, and if you got wet, you had to go home.

"Otherwise, whatever part of your body got wet would fall off if it got too cold."

That's what the man at the carnival told her and Johnny when they were trying to win pencil erasers last summer.

The little kids in the neighborhood were usually sissies, so they went over to Sissy Hill. It was the smallest hill, so all the little kids liked to sled there, and a lot of them even slid down on their butts.

Josephine wouldn't waste her time trying to have fun over there. She would rather have frog warts than try to ride Sissy Hill. That's what the kids called it because it wasn't fast at all. The big kids went to Gobbler's Hill, and that's where the fun was. At least, it was for Josephine.

She loved flying down the hill. She always took her cap off before going down so she could feel the wind pull her hair back and she could brush it at the same time she was going down the hill.

The reason why the kids all called it Gobbler's Hill was because of the creek at the bottom of it. The hill was so fast that if you made it to the creek, it was going to gobble you whole. And if a kid made it to the creek, they might get soaked after falling through the ice. When it was cold out, that meant you were done for the day.

The snowy flakes cleared from the air as Josephine passed the trees that lined both sides of the street as she walked in the middle of it dragging her sled. It wasn't so cold out you couldn't put your tongue on a metal porch swing, but she had no intentions of using her tongue to find out.

This morning she made sure to look into the mirror before she got dressed just to make sure nothing was blue.

This is all because of Johnny's turd face, she thought as she continued to dredge through the thick snow as she tried to get to the top of the hill first.

She wanted to be the first to go down the hill because getting up in the morning wasn't good for you. So if she could get to Gobbler's Hill before anybody else, getting up early would be worth the wear on her eyeballs.

She looked over as she got closer to the top of the hill and could see the kids had begun to gather over on Sissy Hill. That was fine with her. She would have the hill all to herself, and now she was glad that she had dragged her feet out of bed this morning.

After she made it to the top of Gobbler's Hill, it wasn't long before she had gotten a couple of good trips down the hill. She was the first to flatten the snow.

Before she knew it, all the Sissy Hill kids began making their way over to her hill.

"This is Josephine's Hill, and you need permission to go down, or I'm going to push you into the creek," Josephine said to a boy who had dredged his way up the hill to the top where she was standing with her sled in her hand. "Whoever gets to the top of the hill first gets to name it for the day, and that person is me!" She poked herself in the chest.

"Then you're just going to have to push me because I'm going down the hill because it's not your hill!" The boy gave her a dirty look and stared at her.

Josephine stood and stared at the boy and pointed over to the top of the hill where she wanted him to sit on his sled. He probably didn't think that she had the strength to push him far, but she would show him if he didn't think so.

"Get on your sled," she said to him.

Josephine watched as he walked over and placed his sled at the top of the hill and got on it. The boy began to sitting there and waiting for her to give him a push.

"Hurry up, I'm ready!" the boy yelled back at Josephine.

Josephine began to walk further and further away from him. She stopped and turned around and looked at the boy sitting on his sled.

"Okay," Josephine said as she began an all-out sprint right at the boy's back.

He sat there and waited and waited, and then she hit him. He went flying over the top of the hill with the rope clutched in his hand, trying to hold the sled underneath him as he thrust forward off the hill.

As he was launched forward, the air beneath his sled made the first few feet of his journey silent. But then the sled slammed into the snow as he flew downward toward the creek below.

On his way down the hill, his knit cap blew off his head, and his hair began a march away from him as the wind that barreled past him grabbed it as it went by.

He tried to scream, frightened by the speed, but trying to keep the sled underneath him took away his ability to make sound.

Up and down he slammed into the snow as the sled left the surface and slammed him back down.

Then the boy saw it. Coming straight at him was the lip of the hill just before you got to the creek. At the bottom of the hill, the boy saw the creek reaching out its claws and waiting to pull him off his sled and into its murky depths.

As he made it to the bottom of the hill, he let go of the sled as it hit the edge of the creek bed. He was launched straight up into the air. His sled began flying toward the other side of the creek. All the boy could see was a blue sky above him, and it welcomed his upwardly thrown body as it became limp.

Then he began to spin and started falling straight down. He got lucky because he landed on his feet and only his boots got wet. If he had landed any other way, he would probably be done playing for the day because his suit would be soaked with water. But then both of his boots began to fill with water. The boy's face got red as he looked down to see muddy water covering his boots.

He pulled one foot out of the water and then the other. He turned to look up at the top of the hill, and there was Josephine standing at the top of the hill, screaming, "How's the creek, turd face!"

Chapter 6

Martha knew that her mother was unhappy. She was smart, and she could tell when her mom was mad and when she was sad and all kinds of stuff. Like how she cried when she was sad.

Sometimes her mom said she was happy when she cried, but she didn't understand how that could be possible. Could people cry when they were happy?

She would have to ask Timmy that very question. Sometimes kids don't know what they don't know, but she is sure that she knows that. She has to try to be smarter than Timmy, and that is of utmost importance.

Martha didn't know why her mother was unhappy, and sometimes she thought it was her that made her mother unhappy. Martha didn't understand it was never her that made her mother unhappy.

It was because her mother wanted to do more for her than she could. It was part of the reason she was unhappy. But Martha had a suspicion that the grocery store had something to do with it. Every time her mother left the store, she was always upset, and Martha could never figure out why.

She didn't know a lot about grown-up stuff, and her mom cried a lot. As a kid, you can't always be sure that you're not the reason why your mom is crying. Even Martha knows kids are butt pains.

But Martha didn't think it was fair that her mom got to go on roller coasters without her. Her mom said they are emotional roller coasters, but Martha doesn't care what kind of roller coaster it is as long as it's a good one.

She likes the ones with ponies or the ones with horses that go in circles. If she could run around in circles on a horse all day, she would love to, as long as she could take Miss Molly with her.

She couldn't take Miss Barb because she would never be able to ride an emotional rollercoaster with just one arm. She would never be able to hold on.

Martha decided that if she ever got a chance to go on one, she was going to try hard to be brave. That's what's needed to ride one. That's what she overheard her mom say in the kitchen one day.

She thought that maybe if she wasn't here with her mom, then she would be happier and not cry so much. And maybe she wouldn't have any bills. Her mom always says that kids are very expensive, and the more you have, the broker you are.

"You can sell me, Momma," Martha told her mother one night when she came down for a snack and saw her crying. She walked over to her mother and sat down next to her and hugged her and told her mother she "loved her more than all the candy bars in all the world!"

"But if you do sell me, Momma, make sure that they are rich people so I can make big statues out of the bushes."

In front of the house, they had big bushes. Every year her mom let her decorate them however she wanted. So Martha trimmed them and cut them and made them into the shapes of pigs.

"Aren't they sow nice, Momma?" she said to her mother as she showed her the chopped-up bushes. Martha put on a display of the pride and hard work she put into them.

"What are they supposed to be, dear?" her mother said to her.

"They're pigs, Momma!" Martha declared.

"They are beautiful piglets, Martha Morris," her mother said to her and turned around and went back in the house.

Martha looked out her bedroom window and watched as the snow slowly raced across the surface.

Snowdrifts rose through the night, and everything facing her in the distance had a curvature of snow climbing up it. She saw the birds in the trees that chatted back and forth up high. They were displaced by thin piles of snow the length of every branch.

Martha thought the birds were probably bossing each other around as she listened to them in their back-and-forth gesturing.

"Get over there and make a nest!" the girl bird began chirping at the boy bird.

The boy bird turned away from her and began pecking at the branch, wanting to send his ever-chirping partner on a downward dive.

Martha liked birds, but what she loved were butterflies. The way they rose and fell in an almost instantaneous motion. Her mother said she would teach her about the birds and the bees one day, but Martha told her mother she didn't care about the birds and the bees, she just wanted to know about butterflies.

Martha was so glad it was a snow day. She was bored with Miss Beaker, her teacher at school. She always told them the same thing over and over again.

She could only hope that she and Miss Molly would be able to spend the day together. If Miss Molly has to go to work today, they aren't going to be able to play at all. If Miss Molly does go to work, then maybe she will go to Sissy Hill and slide down the hill with Timmy a few times.

If Miss Molly doesn't have to work today, then the two of them are going to play all day together, and while the two of them are playing, they are going to have some more humble pie to make her bones strong.

While she and Miss Molly are reading the morning paper, she is going to try to talk Miss Barb into at least trying to do the dishes.

She told Miss Barb last night before bed, "Miss Barb, I know you only have one arm, but you should at least try to wash the teacups."

Miss Barb replied to Martha that she didn't know how to do the dishes with just one hand. How would she wash them if all she could do is hold them?

Martha looked at Miss Barb aghast. "Miss Barb, how are you ever going to be able to go to work like Miss Molly if you don't try!"

Miss Molly was a dream chaser, but Miss Barb was becoming lazy now that she only had one arm. Martha knew a good dream chaser always had at least one dream catcher.

She figured anyone who had a dream catcher in their home must be a dream chaser. Martha didn't have one yet, but if she tried hard enough, maybe she could get a dream catcher someday if she decided to chase dreams when she grew up.

"You have to run fast to chase your dreams, Miss Molly!" Martha said as she pointed at the doll's face with her finger to make sure she knew she meant business.

Sometimes her mother said that that's what people could be when they grew up—dream chasers. But Martha couldn't imagine people that did jobs they didn't like.

How could people go to work and not like their job? she thought.

Martha's mom couldn't work because she has been injured for some time now. But how could someone not like their job? As a grown-up, she was sure they could do anything they wanted to.

Her mom always got to eat her dessert before she had her dinner, but Martha was never allowed to. Her mother always said that as an adult, you can have your cake and eat it too and just before supper if you wished to. Martha couldn't wait to grow up and have cake and get to eat it too. She will always like her job, and if she doesn't like her job, she will get two of them so the chances of her liking her job is better.

Martha was tired of playing with Miss Molly and went downstairs to ask her mother if she could go outside and play in the snow. Her mother made her sit down and eat a bowl of cereal because she was a growing girl and needed to have something in her stomach to play.

She sat down and ate and thought about trying to eat so much that she could barf on the angel killer, but she didn't like the taste in her mouth afterward, and she was full after just one bowl.

Her mom said she didn't care if she went out and played. So after she was done eating, she went into the mud room and began putting on all her winter clothes.

"Don't drink out of Timmy's juice bottle, it has cooties! Your lips will fall off!" her mom yelled at her as she opened the back door to exit into a winter wonderland.

Martha walked out the back door and stepped out into the fresh thick layer of white snow that encompassed everything she saw. Bunny tracks trampled the distance across the yard, and she took in a long breath of cool morning air and let the bright sun warm her face as she looked straight up into the bright blue sky.

She walked down the back steps and cut through the backyard and over the dirt patch where she and the other kids sat and drew in the sand and played in the dirt. It was covered in a thick layer of snow. She thought of it and all the fun she has playing in it as she walked over it.

She made her way through the yard and across the street to where the kids had already begun gathering to slide down Sissy Hill.

She wasn't too interested in going over to Gobbler's Hill because she didn't want to sled with Josephine. She was still mad at her for putting a sign that read, "I'm a turd face" on her back that she wore all day.

Finally, Miss Beaker stopped her in the hall and ripped it off her back and handed it to her. Sure enough in Josephine's handwriting were the words she had been wearing on her back.

She knew it was Josephine because only Josephine says turd face. Martha thinks it's the stupidest word in the world, and she says it all the time!

Because she was still mad, she was going to go over to Sissy Hill and sled with Timmy if he was there. He was always too afraid of the big hill. But Timmy was afraid of everything.

Martha went over to Sissy Hill and went sledding down it several times, but Timmy wasn't there, so she sledded with the other kids. When she saw Josephine leaving Gobbler's Hill in the direction of home, she decided she was going to go over to Gobbler's Hill so she could go fast down the hill.

Johnny and a bunch of other kids were pushing each other off Gobbler's Hill when she finally made it to the top. She didn't want to be pushed, and she told Johnny and the other boys that they better not push her when she gets on her sled.

"We won't push you, Martha," Johnny said as she put her sled down on the top of the hill.

"You better not!" Martha said as she kept her foot on her sled to keep it from going down the hill without her. She stared at the boys who were standing and looking at her waiting for her to get down on the sled so they could be next.

"Come on, guys, let's stand back here," Johnny said as he herded the boys back.

Johnny and the other boys stood watching her from about ten feet away. She watched them for a moment to make sure they didn't move before she sat down on the sled that was waiting for her to get on.

She sat down on the sled and grabbed the rope. She began moving her butt back and forth to inch the sled forward to the top of the hill.

In an instant, Johnny hit her in the back, and she went flying over the top of the hill.

Her hat flew off as she became airborne as she flew off the top of the hill glued to her sled. When she landed, she began speeding down the hill faster than she had ever gone before.

Her pigtails flew out behind her as she grasped the rope tight and pulled it back as hard as she could to stay on. She forgot about the bottom of the hill until it was too late.

Martha was going so fast when she came down the hill that she went straight across the bank and landed in the middle of the ice on the creek. The ice began to crack, and then it broke underneath her. Then she sat in six inches of water in her snowsuit. Before she could get up, her snowsuit filled with water.

When she was able to get up, she walked over to the bank of the creek and took off her wet snowsuit and began dragging it toward home. She looked up to the top of the hill, and there was Johnny, smiling down at her.

"You're an angel killer, Johnny Ingersol!" Martha yelled up the hill at him and dredged her boots through the snow, making her way toward home.

Chapter

7

Timmy loved snow days, but he was going to miss going to school today. If Johnny didn't put tacks under his feet and on his chair, it would be better, but getting to see his friends made the tacks and getting up out of bed worth it.

He liked Miss Beaker's class. She let him answer a lot of questions, and he always tried to get the answers right so she wouldn't bother him when he fell asleep in class. Timmy liked taking naps, and Martha said they made you smarter. He shouldn't believe her all the time, but she is the smartest girl in school.

Today he wanted to enjoy his snow day and have a good time. Maybe some of his pirate friends would meet him at the pirate ship or build a snowman with him. Timmy loved building a snowman, especially with his little sister. But if his little sister couldn't go outside, then his friends were fun to build with too.

He hated when Johnny ran into his snowman after he finished building them though. Johnny would come running straight at it, and Timmy dared not to get in front of him when he was running toward it. He might come out the other side of a flat snowman looking like a human pancake.

Johnny would run as fast as he could right through it. When he crashed into it, the impact would send his snowman's arms and face skyward and then downward into the snow.

Timmy hated seeing the death of his beloved snowman. Every time he got a chance to build a new snowman, Johnny was always crashing into it. It was worth three flat tires for Johnny next summer for sure.

He always kept a good list of what he owed to people. Timmy still owed Martha for four days of itchy butt crack, but maybe over vacation, he could find a way to get her back.

Timmy still owed Johnny a good one for the pickle crack but not even a new pair of blue balls was going to be enough repayment for that embarrassment. Having the school nurse pull a pickle out of your crack was worth much more. But three flat tires next summer wouldn't make him feel any better now if Johnny destroyed his snowman.

Because he didn't get a chance to go out playing in the snow too often, because there never was any, whenever he got to build a snowman, it was a special day for him. He took the time to make sure that it was rounded and smooth.

He would pay particular attention to getting sticks, which looked like hands at the end of it. His mom got him corncob pipes from the get-more-for-a-dollar store.

But as miraculous as his figures always were, and he found it to be fact, none of them were ever Johnny Ingersol-resistant.

Timmy had something special planned for Johnny while they were on Christmas vacation. Timmy couldn't flatten Johnny's tires now because only dummies ride their bikes in the snow.

Timmy planned to take his sled up to Sissy Hill and stay out all day until he got so cold that the only thing that would thaw him out was a cup of cocoa his mom always kept warm on the stove for him and his friends when they were done playing outside.

When his mom said today was a snow day, he was sure to go to bed early because he knew he had to get to the hill first before any of the other kids. That meant he would have to eat breakfast before anybody else because his mother always made him eat breakfast.

His mom had scrambled eggs and French toast cooking on his way down, and he could smell it. The smell drifted through the air on a quest to find his nose, but he had his snowsuit on his mind as he was jumping down the stairs two at a time as he made his way down them.

"Timmy, go brush your teeth!" his mother yelled up at him as he got all the way down to the bottom of the stairs.

"Ugh!" Timmy said as he turned around and looked up at the top of the stairs. Now he had to go back up the stairs. *I am never going to get to put on my snowsuit!* he thought.

Timmy went back up to the top of the stairs but stopped at the top and turned around and stood on the top step. He leaned against the wall and listened to his mother as she rustled with the dishes in the kitchen.

He stood listening as he raised his hand and stuck out his finger. He then shoved it in his nose and began digging without giving any thought to the matter.

After a minute or so of digging, he pulled out his finger, and to his surprise, there was a huge booger stuck to the end of it. Perhaps larger than any booger he had ever seen before. He was shocked at the size of it.

"King Kong boogers!" he declared from the top of the stairs as he thrust his finger outward to show it to the world.

After waiting patiently for the right time it took to brush his teeth, he stuck his hand in his pocket and wiped the booger off his finger and began running down the stairs.

"I brushed my teeth, Mom!" he screamed as he ran down the stairs to the laundry room where his stuff was all neatly arranged on hooks. Gloves on one hook, "Check!" he said as he pulled them off the hook. Snowsuit, "Check!" he said as he pulled it off the hook.

"Come eat your breakfast," he heard his mom say in the kitchen.

His chin dropped down to his chest with frustration of being halted in his tracks.

"Ugh," he said under his breath as he put his gloves back on the hook. "Okay, Mom," Timmy said as he put his snowsuit back on the hook.

He went into the kitchen and sat down and ate his breakfast while his mother did the dishes, thinking about all the fun he was going to have on his snow day.

After shoveling his food in his mouth, he got up from the table and ran back into the laundry room and grabbed his suit off the hook.

"Come and put your plate in the sink!" his mom called out to him.

He dropped his suit on the floor and dragged his feet back into the kitchen, where she was standing, waiting for him to pick up his plate and hand it to her.

Timmy snatched the plate off the table and walked around the table and handed it to her. Then he turned around as fast as he could and ran to where his suit lay on the floor. He threw on his snowsuit and zipped it up to his chin. His mother would never let him leave the house unless every inch of his body was covered, except for his face.

He didn't like anything on his face, but that was okay because before he could go outside his mother insisted he come see her so she could kiss his cheek before he went outside.

Timmy grabbed his hat and gloves and went to get his mother's kiss and flew out the back door and out into the fresh, thick snow. He stopped as he got halfway across the yard and listened to the silence. He looked up to the blue sky that had become naked of clouds.

There was only the sound of the breeze accompanied by the sound of his boots shoving away the snow in front of him as he began moving forward again. He dragged his feet as he dredged through the snow across the yard to the street, which dead-ended across from Sissy Hill. To his surprise, there were already a lot of kids pushing each other down the hill as gleeful calls of children at play littered the neighborhood with sound.

It was on top of the Sissy Hill that he felt most comfortable. He was so light that if Johnny pushed him down Gobbler's Hill, he would end up in the creek for sure. Johnny loved pushing kids into the creek. Timmy was glad that Johnny had never gotten the chance to push him. He was so small he would end up in the creek for sure.

Timmy looked over as he was standing at the top of the hill after climbing back up and saw Josephine at the top of Gobbler's Hill. Because of Josephine, he decided to take his chances and go over there even if one of the kids on the top of the hill was Johnny. Johnny was always a pest, but there was no doubt that they all did have a lot of fun together.

Timmy began pulling his sled over to Gobbler's Hill, but when he got there, neither Josephine nor Martha were there to greet him and compliment him on his bravery for coming to the top of the hill while Johnny was there.

He was sad and frightened, instantly knowing both of them were gone. As he got to the top of the hill and looked out over the vast white snow that glittered off the surrounding hills, he saw Josephine making her way down the other side of the hill toward home.

Timmy looked down at the bottom of the hill and saw Martha walking along the creek on her way home, dragging her snowsuit behind her. He could tell, because he was so smart, that she wasn't happy to have gotten cold-water bitten.

"Look who it is. It's the smartest kid in class," Johnny said as he pointed at Timmy.

"It's your turn, smart kid," a kid said as he pointed to a spot at the crest of the hill.

Another boy urged Timmy to come over with his sled and get on it. He looked at Timmy and smiled and pointed to the spot where he wanted Timmy to put his sled down.

Timmy resisted going over to the top of the hill and setting his sled down with all the bigger boys watching him. Johnny just stood there and glared at Timmy with trouble displayed on his face.

"I don't want to be pushed!" Timmy yelled out at the boys as they all watched him.

Timmy slowly dragged his sled over to the top of the hill where all the boys were looking.

"Don't push me!" he said as he set his sled down and got on.

He scooched his butt a couple of times to move the sled forward, but he was having a hard time getting it to move with his snowsuit on.

In an instant, Johnny slammed into his back, and Timmy went flying off the top of the hill and began flying down the hill. His hair began flying straight back, and then he felt it. That warm feeling between your legs when you let it all go.

Timmy's mouth was wide open the whole way down the hill. He tried to scream, but his throat would not push anything out of his word hole.

He was so mad when he finally started approaching the bottom of the hill, but as he got closer and closer to the creek, he wasn't slowing down.

Then all of a sudden he was airborne as he hit the lip of the creek, and down he came into the water where the ice had been broken from someone else going down before him. Then his boots and snowsuit began to fill with water.

His anger at Johnny exploded as he got up off his butt. He grabbed his sled and started walking up the hill as if he were going to rip off Johnny's arm and beat him with a bloody stump.

Timmy got almost to the top of the hill when he looked up to see all the boys at the top of the hill looking down at him.

At the top of his voice, Johnny screamed, "Snowball fight!" At the same moment, he pointed at Timmy.

All the boys reached down to the ground to pick up snowballs, but Johnny already had one in his hand he had been packing the whole time Timmy was dredging up the hill.

Before the kids ever got a chance to make a snowball, Johnny unleashed his snowball toward Timmy. Timmy looked up only in time to see the snowball before it hit him in the mouth.

To his horror, Timmy saw his front tooth come flying out of his mouth and land in the snow. Then he looked up again to see a bunch more snowballs coming straight at him. When they impacted, Timmy lost his balance and fell backward and began sliding down the hill.

Timmy slid down the hill on his back for what seemed like forever. When he finally came to a stop, he lay there, and then he tasted blood in his mouth. He probed the inside of his mouth with his tongue only to find a huge gap where his front tooth had been.

The gap where his tooth used to be felt huge as he probed it with the tip of his tongue. The pain in his lip from where the snowball hit him felt like his upper lip had the worst wedgie chaff kind of feeling. Only it was a snowball that had chaffed him.

At the top of the hill, the rest of the boys began getting on their sleds, and that's when Timmy's horror got his heart beating out of his chest.

Timmy jumped up from the ground and put his hands up in the air to stop the boys.

"Don't run over my tooth!" he began screaming with desperation. "Don't run over my tooth, don't run over my tooth! I need it for the fairy!"

Then all at once they came over the top of the hill on their sleds—right toward him.

Chapter 8

Johnny lay in his bed dreaming about the new bike his mom was getting him for Christmas. If he went and saw Santa, he could ask him for a bike, and he could ask for a new racetrack and some army men from his mom, but he didn't want to go see Santa.

Santa was stupid, and Johnny wanted a bike and didn't want to go and sit on a fat man's lap to ask him for one. He just wanted his mom to give him one. And when he got up Christmas morning, there better be a new bike for him, or he wasn't ever going to do another chore again.

He looked out the window as the large snowflakes went by on their way down to make a pile below it. He was excited it was a snow day today. He knew he was going to have fun picking on the kids for using the Sissy Hill, and that was just the start of his day.

He thought of getting up and going downstairs to put on his snow gear and go out and play now, but he knew if he went downstairs, his mother would make him do chores, and he hated chores.

"Johnny, would you please clean your room before you come down, please?" he heard his mother scream up the stairs to him.

Johnny got up from his bed and walked over to the door and finished pulling it the rest of the way open.

"I'm not cleaning my stupid room!" he screamed out into the hall and slammed the door closed.

With the urgency of an ant on a sugar pile, he threw on a pair of pants and a shirt. He thought no kid should ever have to do chores.

Being a kid was for having fun and not going to stupid school and cleaning his stupid room. But he did like having a lot of kids to pick on every day at school.

If you're a kid, you should be able to do anything you want to do. You shouldn't have to listen to parents telling you what to do all the time or cleaning or anything else that distracts a kid from what's important.

Having fun, that's what's important. It's what being a kid is all about. Only parents should have to clean. Kids shouldn't be told what to do when they get home from school either. School is a lot of work, and he didn't think any kid should have to work at home after a hard day at school.

Johnny was exhausted every day trying to make kids mad or getting them to cry. He had to think hard; and when he got home, he wanted to sleep, not clean his room. That's what his mother is for. When he gets home from school, he should be free of chore struggles.

When Johnny grew up, he was going to live with his mom because he would never be able to cook for himself. When he grew up, he was never washing dishes either, and he was always going to make sure to have his dessert before dinner. That was going to be one of his grown-up rules when he was big.

If he had kids, he was never going to tell them what to do. He didn't like being told what to do, so he would never tell his kids what to do. But he didn't think that he was going to get a wife when he grew up because he would have to kiss a girl every day. He couldn't imagine anything worse than having to kiss a girl every day!

Johnny was excited about making his way over to Sissy Hill to pick on the little kids. He didn't like getting to the hill too early because there wouldn't be any kids for him to pick on, so he wasn't in a rush.

He loved picking on the little kids at the little hill, but he liked picking on all the kids on Gobbler's Hill even more. If he got a chance, he would make the creek gobble the kids up.

Today he was going to do things a little differently. Today he was going to dredge up Gobbler's Hill and push everybody down the hill he could. Maybe he could even get someone into the creek. Johnny tried pushing kids into the creek, but the kids stopped themselves before they got to the bottom. Sometimes with their feet, other times by throwing themselves off their sled. Abandoning ship on their way down the hill.

Johnny made his way up to Gobbler's Hill. When he got there, Josephine was at the bottom of the hill and dredging her way back up to the top, but when she saw him standing at the top of the hill with a big smile on his face, she turned in another direction and started walking home.

Martha came up the hill, and he told her he wouldn't push her, but Johnny just couldn't resist the urge and barreled into the back of Martha, sending her flying off the edge.

After he hit her in the back, she went flying down the hill faster than anyone Johnny had ever seen. When she finally stopped in the middle of the creek, he could almost hear the ice crack from where he was standing on the top of the hill. He was so excited he pushed her into the creek that he began jumping for joy.

Johnny stood on the top of the hill smiling and looking down at her as she screamed, "Stupid angel killer!" over and over again as she walked home.

A few minutes later, Timmy showed up, and Johnny couldn't believe his luck. Timmy was so small that he could hit the creek with him for sure if he hit him hard enough. Sure enough, Timmy went flying down the hill. To his surprise, when Timmy climbed out of the creek, he began making his way back up the hill.

Johnny reached down and began making a superduper hard snowball to throw at him on his way up, but he was going to wait until he was almost back up to the top of the hill before he launched it.

Timmy slowly made his way back up the hill, dragging his wet frozen feet and his sled behind him. When he got nearly to the top, he looked up, and Johnny screamed out, "Snowball fight!" and Johnny launched the ice ball down at Timmy.

The ball hit him right in the mouth as he looked up, and Johnny saw Timmy's tooth come flying out of his mouth. At the same time, the kids standing next to him unleashed snowballs directly aimed at Timmy. With the impacts of the snowballs, Timmy lost his balance and fell backward and slid back down the hill.

Johnny stood on top of the hill, laughing and pointing down at him as he lay there. When Timmy looked back up the hill at Johnny, Johnny began screaming down at Timmy, who was boiling with anger at the bottom of the hill.

"That's for the blue balls!" Johnny began to scream.

Before Johnny jumped on his sled, he could hear Timmy down at the bottom of the hill yelling, "Don't run over my tooth!"

Then all the boys at once jumped on their sleds, and over the edge, they went.

It was a fun day for Johnny on the top of Gobbler's Hill, but he was sad that he didn't get to kill any snow angels or run into any snowmen that waved all evening to the eyeballs of the night driving by.

When Johnny finally made it home after a hard day of play, his feet were tired, and he wanted to get his snowsuit off and go upstairs to play with his army men.

Johnny went into the kitchen and ate the supper his mom left for him on the table and then the doorbell rang.

"Johnny? Will you answer the door for me, please?" his mother said from upstairs in her bedroom.

"Ugh!" he said as he slammed his fork down.

Johnny got up from the kitchen table and walked to the front door and opened it. It was Martha.

"Johnny, I need to use your bathroom. I need to poop, and I don't think I'll make it home. It's going to fly out!"

Chapter

9

Josephine loved her snow day. After sledding and making snow angels, and even building a snowman in her front yard, she was so exhausted she went home at the end of the day and went to bed without even eating any supper.

Before she fell asleep, she began to think about Santa. The sun went down, and the lights in the neighborhood began to illuminate the night with bright colors that gleamed across the glass of her bedroom window.

She hoped her mother wasn't going to make her go see Santa this year. She hated going and sitting on the fat man's lap. She always had to get her picture taken with him for her mother, and she never took good pictures. Pictures always made her look like a ghoul. And just because you sat on his knee didn't mean he was going to bring you a present.

How stupid is that, she thought.

She never believed in Santa because the presents downstairs were always written, "To Josephine from Santa," in her mother's handwriting. Every kid knows what their parents' handwriting looks like, and Josephine knew that Santa was sleeping in the room below her. Therefore, she didn't want to waste time going to see Santa if she could get some good sleep instead.

Josephine hoped a new snowstorm would come so she wouldn't have to go to school again before Christmas vacation, but before the birds began to call each other outside of her bedroom window, her mother began to call from the bottom of the landing.

"Josephine? It's time to get up, honey. The bus will be here in thirty minutes. Shake a tail, feather girl! It's your last day of school, and then you will be on vacation!"

"Ugh!" Josephine said to herself as she pulled off her covers and marched over to her bedroom door. She pulled the door open and began yelling down the stairs.

"I don't want to go to school!" she said with fury in her voice.

She slammed the door shut and walked over to her dresser and began pulling out clothes to wear for the day.

"Don't forget to brush your teeth!" her mother screamed up to her.

"Ugh!" Josephine said as she dressed and made sure she had all of her treasures in her pockets.

Having brushed her teeth, she made her way downstairs to the kitchen where her mother had breakfast waiting for her. A brown paper sack that contained her lunch for school sat next to it.

She ate her breakfast and jumped up from the table and grabbed the paper sack off the table. At the same moment, she heard the school bus come around the corner.

Ooh no, she thought.

Josephine dreaded being late for the bus stop because she didn't want to be last in line. If she was last in line it meant landing in a snow pile or even a puddle if it rained. She hated being wet on the school bus in the morning, so every morning she tried to be first in line, but getting her legs to work fast in the morning was so much work.

"Honey, they are having a Christmas Wonderland at the mall while you're on Christmas vacation, so we are going to go see Santa first thing Sunday morning. I want to get a picture of you with Santa."

"Ugh!" Josephine screamed as she ran for the front door, dreading being last at the bus stop.

Her mom had now sent her on a pathway of day destruction. She would be dreading going to see Santa. Being watched by all those people while she sat and begged for something for Christmas?

"Ugh, I hate going to see Santa!" she screamed out to her mother as she ran out the front door and down the front steps to where the bus was parked down the street.

She was so mad at her mother for telling her that. She was so mad she almost fell down the front stairs when running down them. She didn't want the bus to leave without her because her mother would make her walk to school.

"Now my whole last day of school is ruined!" she yelled out as she ran down the street.

Josephine couldn't believe she now had to come up with something to ask for from Santa. If she has to go, she might as well get something good for having to get out of bed, she figured. She does hope there aren't elves running everywhere like there were the last time her mother took her.

Josephine began running down the street only to find out that she would have to stand in line behind Marty.

He's a turd face, she thought.

As she stood there waiting to board the snow train to Miss Beaker's class, Johnny ran up and stood behind her. Josephine turned around and gave him a dirty look.

"Don't you dare, Johnny Ingersol!" Josephine said to him before she turned back around to start climbing the stairs.

Josephine moved forward to the steps, but as she reached them, Johnny grabbed her from behind and pulled her back like he did every morning. He took cuts and began making his way up the stairs in front of her.

As she began to climb the steps, Johnny stopped in front of her, bringing her to a stop on the bottom stair. As she stood there, Johnny began moving forward but reached back without letting the bus driver see him and shoved her backward right into a huge snow pile.

She lay there in the snow pile in disbelief that Johnny Ingersol had gotten her again.

"Josephine Macdonald!" the bus driver said as she looked down as Johnny's big body walked past her. "You get up out of that snow pile right now. I've had enough of you playing every morning when you are supposed to be getting on the bus!"

Every morning she got thrown off the bus by Johnny Ingersol and under the bus by the driver. Josephine threw up her hands in despair as she looked up at the bus driver.

Her flapping jaws and her large bouncing earrings stayed in motion as the driver glared down at her and chewed her gum.

"You wouldn't want this bus to accidentally get a rollin' and run over you and cut you in half now, would you?" the bus driver said as Josephine jumped up and ran onto the bus.

As she sat in Miss Beaker's class, she fumed a few rows over from Johnny. She was going to get him one day. It might not be tomorrow, it might not be Christmas vacation, but she would.

Josephine glared across the classroom at Martha. Martha was always the smartest kid in class; and she watched as her and Timmy, the stupidest kid in class, raced to raise their hands to be first to be able to answer a question for Miss Beaker. It drove her nuts watching the two of them.

Sometimes Miss Beaker would make them go up and write on the chalkboard.

Who, forever sake, would ever want to go up in front of people and write on the chalkboard? Josephine thought as she watched the two of them.

The last day of school before Christmas vacation was her favorite. She would have twelve days in a row to sleep in, and she couldn't wait.

Tomorrow is going to be so warm that she could ride her bike with shorts on, she thought as she began to stare out the window. *From snow day to summer.*

She was glad she was going to be able to stay in bed and never have to move unless her mom made her get up and do her chores.

Chores were almost as bad as school, but at least with chores, she could pretend to do them and tell her mom she was done and sneak out of the house to play.

Sitting in Miss Beaker's class all day today was going to be the longest day of her life. All day today she was going to have to think about the fat man's lap—and pictures.

She was constantly trying to look across the room to see outside the window so she could go into la-la land to forget she was in class. But instead, she had to look over at Martha and her pigtails, who was trying to raise her arm faster than Timmy.

Miss Beaker jabbered on and on, and it was all she could do to keep from looking around. She looked back at Johnny to call him a turd face with her lips, but he was too busy trying to slide tacks up to Timmy's desk with his feet under the chair in front of him.

She finally had some excitement as she watched Timmy moving his bare feet around under his desk, barely missing a tack on the floor pointing upward. She was hoping that she would be able to see the look on Timmy's face when he stuck his bare foot on one of the pointy things under his desk. Then he stepped on it.

She began to laugh, but it was too loud, and it got Miss Beaker's attention, which was one of the last things that she wanted. But Miss Beaker looked around for a moment and then continued to jabber.

Miss Beaker had a bag of kid poison in her top desk drawer, and she knew it. She has never seen it, but she told Johnny that it was there, and now he expects her of all people to go into her desk drawer and prove it.

"All the kids know it's there. Why should I have to prove it?" Josephine said to Johnny.

"Because you're the smartest in the class, so you would do it better than anyone else!" Johnny proclaimed to her. "If you said it, you have to prove it. So when Miss Beaker leaves the class, you have to go up there and find it. You're not a real girl if you don't."

Josephine huffed and puffed, but she was going to prove her girlhood. And yes, she was the smartest girl in class because she can put up with Martha. That means she can do something nobody else can and that makes her the smartest.

"Class, I have to go to the bathroom, so I will be right back," Miss Beaker said at the front of the class.

Johnny fixated a look on Josephine as she looked over at him, and then he began to smile. His hands began to move about. He started waving at her and talking under his breath, but she couldn't understand what he was saying halfway across the room.

The door slammed as Miss Beaker left the room, and Josephine didn't want to get up, but she had to. She had to see it. It was there in her top drawer, and she knew it. Thirty seconds, that's all she needed to look, and with that, Josephine got up from her chair.

Johnny sat in the back of the class, and his mouth fell open when Josephine got up from her chair and began walking up to Miss Beaker's desk.

She is going to do it! Johnny thought. His butt began to lift off his chair as his excitement grew.

Josephine made her way up to the front of the class and reached over the top of the desk and slowly began to open Miss Beaker's top desk drawer. And there it was—staring straight at her. A plastic bag with a piece of masking tape on it that read, "*Kid Poison.*" She froze in place and just stared at it.

In the back of the room, Johnny couldn't take it and got up from his seat. He ran up to the desk where the drawer sat open and Josephine was staring down at it.

He looked over the top of the desk and down into the drawer, only to see what Josephine was staring at with horror. He had seen it with his own two eyes. *Kid Poison!* He hated it when Josephine was right. He huffed as he looked at Josephine and turned around and began running back to his desk.

Josephine shut the drawer and ran back over to her desk and sat down. The look on her face was the same one Johnny had on his when she looked back at him. Sheer terror.

"We are going to die!" Josephine said to Johnny without making a sound.

"I know!" he said back to her silently.

After waiting patiently for what seemed like forever to the children, who began to get restless and started to verbally stir, Miss Beaker walked in and went straight to her desk.

"Did everybody fill out their Christmas cards to hand out to each other? It is the last day of school before your Christmas vacation, and it's time to spread some friendly cheer to your classmates!" Miss Beaker said as she reached into her top desk drawer.

Instantly, Josephine and Johnny tensed in their chairs as they watched her pull out a small plastic bag. It was filled with small Christmas cards she had filled out for the children.

"Okay, children, take out the cards that you wrote for each person in the class and place them on the desk of each of your classmates."

All the children in the classroom began to shuffle about as they pulled little cards out of baggies and placed them on their classmate's desks.

After all the kids sat down, Miss Beaker told them they could have ten minutes to read through the cards their classmates gave them.

Josephine sat at her desk and began picking through the Christmas cards the other kids had set on her desk. When she got the Christmas card from Johnny, she opened it and read what it said, and she got so mad as she looked over to see him smiling at her.

She looked down and read it again.

"Have a blue nipple Christmas! Johnny."

All she could think of at that moment was how she would love to squeeze out a tube of toothpaste into his crack.

She fumbled through the cards to find the one Timmy had written for her. Of course, Timmy was the only kid that didn't put his name on the card. That's how she knew it was from him.

Timmy is so stupid, she thought as she rushed to get the card open.

When she opened up the card and read it, she looked up at Timmy, and he was smiling at her, and then all of a sudden, Timmy jerked backward in his chair.

"Ouch!" Timmy screamed out, but Miss Beaker must not have heard him. Timmy began digging at his toes to pull out a tack that stabbed him between his toes. She looked at Johnny, and he was laughing. Johnny was laughing so hard Josephine thought he was going to pee his pants.

She looked down at the card from Timmy and read it again. It simply read, *"I love you, Merry Christmas."* Josephine slipped the card into her pocket with her rabbit's foot and began shuffling through the rest of her cards.

She finished opening all of her cards, and the last card was from Martha. She picked the card up and opened it and began to read.

"Give me Miss Barb's arm back! She has to do the dishes! Merry Christmas, Martha."

Chapter 10

Martha wished her mom was going to have a good day. Martha watched her as she struggled at the kitchen sink, trying to do the dishes. It was hard for her mother to stand for too long, and Martha wishes she could do the dishes for her, but she hates doing dishes.

My mom does it better anyway, Martha thought.

She ate her breakfast and grabbed her lunch bag off the counter and kissed her mother goodbye.

"I love you, Momma!" she said as she began racing for the front door. She wanted to be early to the bus stop so she could be first in line.

Martha made her way to the front door while trying to get her backpack on. She opened the front door to a welcoming view of white piles of snow that guided her path down the sidewalk and to the street where the children had begun to gather for the bus. But now it was all going to melt.

Their snowman will become puddleman. Martha was sad about their snowman. However, at least it will be the first to be Johnny Ingersol-resistant.

Martha was so mad. Timmy was already standing at the bus stop when she looked to see who was already waiting. Her shoulders slumped, and her backpack slid off her shoulders and landed right on the back of her ankle.

"Ouch!" she proclaimed as she began limping her way to the bus stop.

She began to think about Santa and what it was she wanted for Christmas, but she just couldn't decide. She thought of asking Miss Molly what she should ask for, but all Miss Molly wants to do anymore is have pity parties.

Martha doesn't want to have those kinds of parties anymore, and she doesn't like humble pie anymore either. She had enough of that. She just wished Miss Barb could drink tea with her again soon.

She was so excited she was going go to the Christmas Wonderland at the mall and even get to sit on Santa's knee this year. She is worried she won't know what to ask for, and the last thing she needs to make right now is a last-minute decision. After all, cookies are hard enough to make.

Her mom said they couldn't afford it, but she would find a way to take Martha regardless of how much money they had.

Martha just hoped she would be able to get there first. Her mom doesn't move around too fast, so she hoped she wouldn't have to race her mom against Timmy's mom to be first in line.

When she got to school, all she could think about was Santa and the elves that were going to be there. She wanted to see Santa, but she desperately wanted to see the elves. Her mother calls them little people, and Martha doesn't think they are people at all. They're magical.

"Martha!" Johnny tried to scream quietly.

"Martha!" Johnny kept calling again and again until she finally looked over at him.

"Shhh!" Martha said back to him. "You're going to get us into trouble!"

She was listening to Miss Beaker and wanted her to finish the lesson so they could get to the part of the day where they could pass out Christmas cards to each other. If Johnny caused a fuss and got her into trouble, she was going to get him.

Johnny looked over at her, desperately trying to get her attention with something of importance that he must convey to her.

"Martha! You're going to die!" Johnny said with a look of horror on his face. "Miss Beaker got kid poison on her hands and got it on the toilet that you used!" Johnny pointed at her. "You're going to die!"

Martha sat and stewed. "Shut up, angel killer!" Martha said as Miss Beaker turned around and looked at the class.

"Who was that?" Miss Beaker said with a deep voice.

Martha sat and thought about whether it was possible to die from kid poisoning if it was on the toilet seat when you sat on it. Then she thought of every time she put itching powder on someone's toilet, and…"Oh my god!" Martha gasped to herself. "I'm going to die of toilet seat poisoning!"

Martha stared at Miss Beaker as she scanned the kids in the front row and began looking across the second row. Martha shot her hand up into the air as Johnny looked over at her and glared at her.

"I know who it was, Miss Beaker!" Martha called out in her know-it-all voice. She pointed over at Johnny and said, "It was Johnny Ingersol!"

Everyone in the class turned and started staring at Johnny as his face grew a deep red.

"Johnny Ingersol!" Miss Beaker said slowly as she began to walk around her desk and to his row of desks. "At the end of class today, you will come up and write twenty-five times on the board, *'I will not make fun of blue-nippled Eskimos!'*"

If Martha could have, she would have gone over and put her hand on the floor so when Johnny's jaw hit it, the pain would be far less. But Johnny deserved a good knuckle to the chomper, Martha figured.

Johnny looked over at Martha and watched her as her lips moved.

"I told you so!" Martha said to him without uttering a sound.

Martha was so excited to hand out the little square Christmas cards to everybody when Miss Beaker said they could all trade. When Martha started handing out cards, she didn't want to put one on Josephine's desk, but she did.

After Martha handed out all her cards, she went back and shuffled through the pile of names. She grabbed the one that said "Johnny" on it and opened the little envelope.

Written inside the card was, *"How was the creek? Merry Christmas, Johnny."* Martha turned in Johnny's direction and stuck her tongue out at him, even though he wasn't paying attention because he was busy shooting spitballs at Timmy.

Martha shuffled through the little pile of cards looking for a name that she would like to hear from. Then she saw the little card from Josephine. She picked up the little card and opened it and began to read it. On it, Josephine wrote, *"Merry Christmas, turd face!"*

Martha looked across the room at Josephine hoping to be able to stick her tongue out at her, but she was busy reading the cards of her own.

When she got the card from Timmy, she opened it and read what he had to say to her. When she read it, she giggled. It read, *"I win! Merry Christmas!"*

At the end of the day, Martha was exhausted when she got home. At supper, and not long before she went to bed, something was bothering her. She desperately wanted to ask her mother, but she just couldn't bring herself to. But then she just blurted it out.

"Momma?" she asked her mother as she began cleaning the dishes from the table.

"Yes, honey, what is it?" her mother said as she began filling the sink with water.

"Can you die if there is poison on the toilet seat and you sit on it?" Martha said as she sat and stared and waited for the answer that was merely a matter of life or death.

"Of course, dear!" her mother said as she dropped a plate, shattering it and scaring Martha half to death.

Chapter 11

Timmy couldn't believe it when his mother told him that he was going to see Santa and get to go and sit on his knee of all things and he was even going to get to ask Santa for anything he wanted.

He was going to see elves, and he was going to see Santa! Santa was going to have a real reindeer with him, and Timmy's excitement couldn't be greater. Timmy wasn't sure of the name of the reindeer that he was going to bring to town with him, but Timmy was pretty sure that it was going to be Dancer.

His mom said that at Christmas Wonderland, they were going to have elves there, and they were going to be dancing elves.

If Santa was going to be dancing, he would need an experienced reindeer to keep up, Timmy thought.

Dancer, the reindeer, probably had lots of experience dancing. Maybe in a previous reindeer life, Dancer was a ballerina? Timmy knows that he is smart because he figured that out himself.

Josephine and Johnny were arguing as he was walking down the hall to his locker, which was right next to Josephine's and Johnny's. He was always feeling like a turd sandwich because his locker was between the two of them.

"You can't go see Santa, even if you wanted to, because you are going to die from kid poison!" Johnny said to Timmy as he made a thrusting motion as if he were a pirate giving Timmy one final jab with his sword.

"No, I'm not!" Timmy said with fear in his voice as he tried to open his locker.

"Yes, you are! Miss Beaker had kid poison on her hand, and she smacked you on the back five times for doing such a good job on the chalkboard. Being the smart kid is going to make you die dead!"

"You can't die dead!" Timmy declared. "If you die, you're dead!"

Timmy couldn't believe how stupid Johnny was. Even he knew that dying wasn't dead!

"You will be dead long before Santa comes to town! She had kid poison in her top drawer, and she touched it when she stuck her hand in it. You are going to die!"

"You can't die if someone touches you with poison on their hand!" Timmy said with contempt. "They would already be dead! Dummy!" Timmy said with frustration.

Timmy knew it was true. If she had poison on her hand, he was a goner for sure!

Sitting in class, he got to race Martha, and he got to dodge spitballs from Johnny. He didn't mind when Johnny aimed them at him because his favorite part was trying to get Johnny to miss.

When he did miss, the girl in front of Timmy had a spitball convention attended to by many going on in her hair. The girl sitting in front of Timmy sometimes had a bunch of spitballs in her hair from Johnny's misses. But she always got mad at Timmy because she thought it was Timmy playing with it.

Timmy was excited that it was the last day of school before the Christmas vacation. He was glad he was going to finally get to hand out his cards to the other students.

When Miss Beaker said they could all hand out their Christmas cards, Timmy shot out of his seat and began running around the room, putting his little cards on other people's desks.

When Timmy sat down at his desk, he rifled through all the cards to find the one he was looking for. It was the card from Josephine. Timmy began opening the little card from her.

He was hoping by the pitter-patter going on in his chest that she was going to say something in the card that would make his heart beat even faster, but when he read the card, it said, *"Turd face! Merry Christmas, Josephine."*

Timmy slumped down in his chair and began to sulk. Then out of the corner of his eye, he saw the card from Johnny. Timmy reached out and grabbed the card and opened it. It said, *"I found your tooth! Merry Christmas."*

Timmy was so happy he looked back a couple of chairs to Johnny, and all Johnny saw when he looked up at Timmy was a gaping hole where his tooth had once been. Timmy had the largest smile on his face Johnny had ever seen.

Timmy looked down and saw the card from Martha and picked it up. He opened it and began reading. *"Don't emergency poop at my house, it stinks! Merry Christmas, Martha."*

When Timmy got home from school after his last day, he was tired from such an exhausting day. When he was sitting down at the table for supper, he looked over at his mom who was getting up to put her plate in the sink.

"Mom, can you die if someone touches you and they have poison on their hand?"

He wasn't sure if she heard him or not or whether she was contemplating his curiosity about poisons, so he waited as she opened the cupboard door.

"Of course, you can, honey!" his mother said as she slammed the cupboard door closed, startling Timmy.

"Great! Now I'm going to die before I get to go see Santa!" Timmy said as he rose from the table and began to cry.

"No, you won't, dear," his mother said to him as he stomped up to his room to die.

Chapter

12

Johnny did not want to get up for school on his last day. He knew it was his last day, but he still did not want to go to school. He lay in his bed and stared up at the ceiling as every few minutes his mother sent up a bugle call to get him to rise for one final time this year.

He was so mad his mother was going to make him go see Santa. A Christmas Wonderland? All the kids were going to be there, and to make things worse, kids were going to be gleaming up at Santa, and there he would be. Sitting on Santa's lap while all the other kids who had gone before him stared and watched on in disbelief as Johnny kicked Santa in his shin.

What does he want from Santa? He wants Santa to make his mom leave him alone. And a bike. He doesn't care if Santa has to drag it all around the world or his mother has to drag it all over town, he wants one. A white one. It will be like him on a cloud blasting through the air, full of lightning. He was going to be faster than a lightning bolt.

When he grows up, he is going to get his government to pass a new law that says no kid should have to go see Santa unless they want to.

He was going to be so mad when he saw Santa that he was not going to tell him anything when he sat down on his lap. He was going to sit there and stare at him and prove to Santa that he could do whatever he wanted to do. Then he was going to make Santa guess what he wanted for Christmas.

He lay in bed for just a few more minutes. He got up and got dressed and waited for all the kids to be lined up at the bus stop so when he got down there, he would be the last in line. Josephine never wanted to be last in line, but he did.

Johnny ran out the front door with his sandwich bag in his hand. He didn't want the bus to leave without him, but his backpack was holding him back.

When all the kids began starting their way up the stairs onto the bus, Johnny arrived out of breath in line behind Josephine after he had to run down the street. Then he grabbed Josephine and took cuts.

Josephine began climbing the steps behind Johnny. He couldn't see the scowl that was on her face.

That's when Johnny reached back at her with a stiff arm and launched her backward off the bottom step and into a snow pile.

Johnny didn't like school, but he loved everything about school. He got to pick on other kids, and sometimes he even got to make his teachers mad.

He didn't like it when they got so mad that they would send him down to the principal's office though, but just in case, he put a few extra tacks in his pocket in case he was able to slip one onto the principal's chair.

Miss Beaker hated it when he acted silly in class. He knew one of these days she was going to do him in. He was waiting for a dunce cap to come out of one of her drawers one day, and he would have to sit in a corner, but that was one thing he was never going to do. She would have to drag him to the principal's office.

Miss Beaker told them to hand out their Christmas cards; so Johnny, like everybody else, began walking around to other kids' desks to put the Christmas cards on their desk.

After Johnny passed out all his cards and sat down at his desk to look at the pile that arrived while he was away from his desk, he began sifting through them and looking at all the names.

He shuffled through the pile of cards until he got to the one that he was looking for. It said on the front of the envelope, *"From Martha."*

Johnny began opening the little card because he wanted to know what she was going to write to him. When he pulled the card out of the envelope and opened it, a little bit of cream-colored powder came out of the card and fell onto his desk.

Then he read the card. In Martha's beautiful handwriting, she wrote, *"Kid poison for you, angel killer! Merry Christmas, Martha."*

Johnny looked over at Martha and opened the book that was sitting on his desk and, without Martha seeing, pulled out his straw. As Martha turned away to look at her cards, Johnny shot a heavy, wet spitball at her and hit her right in the side of her head, and it hit hard enough to cling to her hair without her knowing. There she sat looking through her cards with a big spitball in her hair.

He kept opening up all his cards until he got to the card from Timmy. He opened up the card and looked over at Timmy, and he had a huge smile on his face.

Written on Johnny's card from Timmy was, *"Where's my tooth, blue balls! Merry Christmas, Timmy."*

Johnny shuffled through his cards and got to the one that had Josephine written across the front of it. He opened the card and began reading.

That's why both my feet slid off the pedals of my bike when I tried riding it! Johnny thought as he read the card from Josephine. "I'm not such a bad driver after all!" Johnny said to himself as he read the writing again and looked over at Josephine with a dirty look on his face.

She looked back at him and stuck her tongue out at him.

On the card it read, *"I tied a knot on your bike chain, so if you tried to ride it, you'd fall on your turd face! Merry Christmas Josephine."*

Then Johnny's arms began to itch.

Chapter 13

Johnny wasn't bored on the first day of his vacation, but finding kids to play with had gotten boring. Johnny walked down the street looking, but there were no kids outside playing.

The snow was melting rapidly, and it was becoming a mud-puddle dream, but only to the brave. If a kid went home with mud on their shoes and got it all over their mother's floor, they might be attacked by a Mother Pirate. The scariest pirate on the seven seas.

Johnny walked along the outside of the playground and saw Timmy standing up on the pirate ship all by himself. No other pirates were tending to the sails or available for a good swift mutiny. Johnny could tell when there was a mutiny on the pirate ship because that's when somebody usually threw Timmy off. It was usually Josephine that threw him overboard though.

Timmy was standing at the helm and slowly moving the wheel back and forth as if he were steering a vessel through a calm and quiet sea. He was standing still and taking in the thought of the soft ocean spray as it slowly dampened his cheeks and forehead.

"Timmy!" Johnny called out as he stood at the edge of the playground, trying to get his attention.

"Timmy!" he called out again as Timmy stopped what he was doing and looked around.

Timmy saw Johnny and stared at him as he kept moving the ship's helm back and forth, slow and steady.

From the edge of the playground, Johnny urgently tried to wave Timmy down and over to where he was standing.

Timmy stopped what he was doing and climbed down from the pirate ship, careful not to fall because he didn't have his snowsuit on and he would get soaked for sure.

"Abandon ship!" Timmy screamed out as he jumped down from the last step.

Being careful where he walked because of the mud, he cut across the playground to where Johnny was standing holding a bottle of bubbles.

"What's that for?" Timmy said as he looked at the bottle in Johnny's hand. "Are we going to blow bubbles?"

"This is magic, Timmy, and I can prove it," Johnny said with confidence as he lifted the bottle of bubbles to show him. "We are not going to pull the plastic thing out and blow bubbles, but you are going to put your tongue in there and get soap on it." Johnny began taking off the lid to the bubbles.

"I'm not putting my tongue in there!" Timmy said as he crossed his arms over his chest.

"Yes, you are. But it will make your tongue fence post immune. Your tongue won't be able to stick with bubble soap on it. Try it!" Johnny said as he pointed to the metal post holding up the playground sign.

Timmy stared at Johnny with a whole lot of doubt in his mind. But then he stuck his tongue out and put it into the bottle of bubble soap. He pulled his tongue out that now had soap on it and stuck it to the metal post.

"It didn't stick!" Timmy said as the relief shot through him that he wasn't going to be just another one of Johnny's squirmers at a metal pole. "It worked! It didn't stick!" Timmy was elated to have learned something new.

"Of course, it didn't stick, dummy! The snow is melting, and it's too warm. I just wanted to see if you'd stick your tongue into a bottle of soap. How does it taste?" Johnny said as he began to laugh and walk away.

Timmy's face got red, and then he began trying to wipe the taste of soap off his tongue as he watched Johnny walk away.

Hello Santa

"Mom, do you think we are going to have a white Christmas this year?" Martha asked her mom as they threaded popcorn on a string. Carefully she guided a needle through each piece of popcorn.

After they were done stringing it all, her mom was going to coat it with caramel so she could have a snack off the tree on Christmas Eve.

"I'm afraid not, dear. It is supposed to get as warm as a summer day for nearly a week. You will get your summer in the winter, Martha Morris," her mother said with glee for having a reprieve from the ice and snow and the cold of all things.

Martha loved having snacks on her Christmas tree. It was so beautiful as she stared at it as she worked. She would have a tree with food on it, and now all she needed to get was a tree for her mom. A tree that grew money on it.

Her mom always said that she didn't have a tree that grew money, so Martha wants to get her one someday. Maybe for Christmas. She guesses they are probably expensive, so she will save her money when she grows up. Then her mom will have a tree that grows money on it, and she can have all the money she wants!

Her mom helps her put things she can eat like candy canes and caramel popcorn on a string on the tree because her mom knows that she likes to walk up to the tree and get a snack. She just wishes the tree could poop presents while it just sat there.

What use is a tree that just sits there and looks good? Martha thought.

Martha liked sitting around and snacking with her mother as they waited patiently for Santa to bring his big butt down the chimney.

If he got soot on his backside, Martha thought, *then Santa might accidentally fart toxic clouds at the elves. The horror!*

Martha wasn't paying attention as she giggled at the thought of it and poked her finger with the tip of the needle that she was shoving through popcorn. It poked her hard enough for her to see a spot of red appear and then begin to grow larger. The joyful look on her face changed to a "*I hate popcorn!*" look.

Martha loved the time she got to decorate with her mom. It only took them ten minutes because all of Mom's preciouses, which is what she called them, were only enough to fill one box. Their tree looked more like a branch with grass glued to it, but her mom made it look like the most beautiful tree in the great big world.

Moms can be great, Martha thought as the two worked together sprucing up the house with decorations and sparkly strands that she allowed Martha to hang from all the curtain rods.

Martha loves sparkles. The glitter strands that her mom let her hang from the tree were her favorite. She would always save a few to put on her momma's head and then tell her how beautiful she is.

"Just because your body is broken, Momma, doesn't mean you aren't the most beautiful mom in the world!" Martha declared. She was tired of shoving the needle through the popcorn.

"Can I go play in the snow before it's all gone, Momma?" she said as she put down the needle that had poked her.

Martha was sad that school had let out for Christmas vacation, but she was also really happy that she was going to get to go see Santa—and to be able to play with her friends, even though Timmy was stupid, Johnny was an angel killer, and Josephine was a jerk.

Martha threw on her jacket and was the first to make it to the playground before all the other children began to arrive. All by herself, she started rolling a snowball to make a snowman. The snow had begun to melt, so it was heavy.

Soon Timmy arrived, and then Josephine showed up with a couple of other kids that went and played on the pirate ship with Timmy. Timmy took his usual place at the helm of the pirate ship.

Martha and Josephine lay down in the snow, and the two of them began to make snow angels together. It was the one thing they truly enjoyed doing together. But there was always a contest to see whose was more beautiful.

When they were done, they both looked down at them to see whose was better.

"Yours looks stupid. I win," Josephine said as she turned around to go and start making a snowman.

Martha and Josephine worked together making two big balls for a snowman. They both took one of the large snowballs and set it on the other. Then they went to work making the third ball, but it was too big and too high for them to lift it. Both of them looked over and saw Johnny coming and then looked at each other and smiled.

"We will get him to do it!" Josephine said to Martha as they both looked at the huge ball sitting on the ground.

Johnny was going to go over to the pirate ship, probably to throw Timmy overboard, but the two of them called to come over and help them.

As Johnny was walking toward them, he saw there were two snow angels in the snow. He saw the smaller angel lying in the snow and began walking through it as he walked to where the two of them stood next to their snowman watching him.

Martha knew before he did it that he was going to walk through her snow angel, and she got so mad. He had walked through her snow angel for the last time!

"You're an angel killer, Johnny Ingersol!" she yelled out at him as he smiled and trampled through it.

Martha wanted to punch him, but she knew that she couldn't hurt him, so she promised to get him one day. She was going to get him good.

"I will get you one day, Johnny Ingersol!"

Johnny picked up the big ball that was sitting on the ground between the two girls and lifted it and put it on the top of the snowman.

"Thank you, Johnny," Josephine said to him as she began working on rounding the balls of snow. Carefully they began to work.

Martha began helping her, and Johnny disappeared and reappeared carrying two perfect sticks for arms.

When they were done, the three of them stood back and began looking at it. Timmy came down from the pirate ship and came over to where the three of them were standing in front of the snowman. The four of them stood there silently, admiring the snowman.

"It's the most perfect snowman ever in the world," Timmy said softly.

Chapter 14

It was early when Martha's mother woke her up.

"It's time to go see Santa, Martha!" her mother yelled up to her from the bottom of the landing.

Her mother said she would get her up early so they could get to the mall and Martha could be first in line. Martha was so excited to see Santa that she would go in her pajamas if she must be the first to see him.

Martha snapped her eyeballs open when she heard her mother begin to call. The excitement instantly began to run through her body.

Martha threw off her covers and ran downstairs without even putting her robe on to see if her momma had her breakfast ready. Her momma said they could leave as soon as she was done eating her breakfast, so she needed to eat extra fast. Martha was going to eat her food so fast that they would have plenty of time, but her mom told her to take her time eating her food.

"You're not a turkey, so don't gobble it up!" her mother said as Martha froze in the act of shoveling scrambled eggs into her mouth.

"Thank you, Mom, for taking me to see Santa and the elves," Martha said as she tried to eat her eggs fast without her mom seeing.

After breakfast, her mother helped her do her hair pretty. Martha had so many curls that even Miss Molly was jealous when she showed her. Her mom helped her get dressed up in her favorite dress, and even put a little bit of her makeup on her so she would feel beautiful around the elves. She was an elf princess. *If they had one of those*, she thought.

Martha knew there were going to be a lot of elves there. That is how she knew that it was going to be the real Santa that they were going to see.

She was so excited to ask Santa for presents, but she still didn't know what she was going to ask for. She did know that she had to know before she got up to see him; otherwise, she may never remember.

Martha was super excited when her mother held her hand through Wonderland to get to the Santa line. There was nobody in line. Martha's feet began to run before she could stop them so she could be first. This was going to be her favorite Santa visit ever. Her mother waved to her as she stood looking up at the huge chair.

She was happy that her mom was able to get them here early enough that she could be first in line. She didn't want Santa to be worn out by all the other kids ahead of her because she didn't want him to forget what she wanted. And what she wanted from Santa was very important.

Martha was standing at the gate at the bottom of the stairs that led up to Santa's chair. The elves were handing out gifts to children and people passing by that were admiring the beautiful Christmas Wonderland. It was everywhere and as far as her eyes could see.

Her mother sat on a bench and looked across the way at her. She stood in line staring at the big steps that led to the large chair that sat the huge man. Martha waited and listened to everything going on around her. She was happy. The smile on her face was that of pure joy.

Then Josephine kicked her in the back of the heel as she sneaked up the ropes and right behind her in line. Martha was frightened for a moment until the pain of Josephine's shoe hitting her. She turned around, and the joy she had been feeling a moment ago was gone.

"Ow!" Martha screamed out at Josephine as she looked back at her with a dirty look on her face.

Then Josephine turned around and greeted Timmy as he arrived in line behind her.

Martha turned away from Josephine.

I am never going to let her come over and play with me and my dolls ever again! Martha thought as she began watching the elves run around some more as they handed out gifts.

Loud Christmas songs began to ring out. It was almost time for the arrival of Santa. Martha was so excited to ask Santa for a present. The biggest one she had ever asked for.

Martha began watching the elves again, but then Josephine pulled the little hairs between her pigtails hard, so hard that Martha almost had tears in her eyes in an instant.

"Stop it!" Martha screamed out as she turned around and scowled at Josephine. "I'm mad at you, Josephine!" Martha said angrily as she turned back around and began watching again as an elf ran up to her and handed her a piece of chocolate. She looked down at it, and there was Santa's face winking at her. "You can't talk to me for the rest of our vacation!" Martha yelled out at her as she stood there looking at her piece of chocolate.

"I'm sorry, Martha!" Josephine said with a snotty tone in her voice. "I won't do it again! It was just a silly sign on your back. All day. Well." Josephine began to feel remorse.

"I'm not talking about the sign on my back, and you're the turd face, and yes, you will do it again!" Martha said with a red face as she looked up at Josephine. "Give me Miss Molly's leg back! How is she ever going to go on an emotional rollercoaster with me if she can't walk?"

Just then the elves pulled Santa from behind a curtain, and there he was. In all his red and white and his big black belt restraining a tidal wave of Santa fat.

Her eyes got big and began to imagine the elves coming to get her to bring her up.

Martha stood there looking up at the humongous man with a big white beard and pink cheeks sitting in a chair on a big platform. He was surrounded by presents, and he didn't have to move a muscle. Elves ran about and helped Santa as he waited for the children.

An elf came running down the stairs as her excitement grew. She was going to tell Santa what she wanted for Christmas.

An elf pulled back the rope and grabbed her hand and ushered Martha up the stairs. She looked out, and her mother was getting ready to take her picture as she made her way up the stairs.

When she got up to Santa, his huge gloved hands reached out for her and pulled her so hard that she had no choice but to land on the man's lap.

Martha looked up into Santa's eyes. It was him. It was Santa. His eyes seemed to be glowing at her. She knew that he was the real Santa. He wasn't one of those bell-ringing fake Santas. When she was looking up into his eyes, they were magical and blue as a blue that she had ever seen. Santa was all she had ever dreamed him to be, and he brought presents!

"Hello, Martha!" Santa said to her as he looked at the name tag stuck to the front of her dress.

"Hello, Santa!" Martha said as she sat on his knee in wonderment at the redness of his robe.

All of a sudden a panic struck her, and her mind went blank. She forgot what she was going to ask him. She was so excited she forgot! How could she forget? The smartest kid in class doesn't forget what she is going to ask for from Santa!

Questions started to go through her head as she stood there without being able to talk. As she sat on his lap and stared into his beautiful eyes, she began to wonder, *Do elves pick out which present you get or does Santa? Does Santa bring you what you want down the chimney, or is he too fat, and that isn't true?*

"What would you like Santa to bring you this year?" he said to her, snapping her out of a daze. Martha sat staring into his wondrous eyes.

She looked at him, and she didn't even see his lips move because there was so much white hair on his face that came down to his chest.

Martha looked up into Santa's eyes and said, "I remember, I want my mom to be happy!" Then she jumped off his knee and ran down the ramp to the exit where her mother stood so proud of her.

Chapter

15

"Josephine, get down here!" her mother yelled up at her for the fifth time. It could have been the tenth time for all she cared.

Then Josephine threw off her covers and marched over to her bedroom door and pulled it open as fast as she could, but the edge of the door went over her big toe and shot pain to her brain.

"Fine!" Josephine screamed out as she tried to get the pain under control. She looked down to see that the edge of the door had ripped a chunk of skin off the top of her toe.

"Great, Mom! Now I have to talk to Santa with a chewed-off toe!" Josephine said and slammed the door shut.

Her mother was so annoying, and she had to put up with her seven days a week! It was just about all she could bear. She couldn't imagine having kids when she grew up because how was she going to put up with them?

It was bad enough she had to put up with Johnny, but her mother was a big drag on her fun time—and her sleep time.

Josephine couldn't believe her mom was making her go see Santa. She told her mom at least a thousand times she didn't want to get up, but here she was driving to the mall on a sleepy Sunday morning.

When she got to the mall, she was excited she was behind Martha, but she would never mention that to Martha. That is strictly secret.

After Josephine got in line, she tripped and accidentally kicked Martha, and then Martha was really mad at her.

She watched Martha as she stood looking at the elves as they ran about dancing. Martha was in awe. She watched her as she looked back and forth, but Josephine had no interest in any of it.

Martha thought she was so smart, and here she was gloating over a man sitting with elves looking like the side of a fire truck. Josephine had to get her attention. She wanted to talk to Martha, but she needed a good excuse.

Then Josephine started to look for something on Martha's dress to pull on.

As Martha stood in front of her, Josephine noticed her dress looked pretty and neatly pressed, as if someone took the time with each ruffle. Martha tried to look pretty, and as Josephine looked closer, she couldn't believe how beautiful and happy Martha looked as she glanced about.

Josephine wasn't jealous of her because she knew that Martha was just Martha. If she just wanted to be an ordinary girl, that was fine with her.

She could tell Martha was excited, but Josephine was so tired. The thought of excitement made her even more tired.

Martha's pigtails danced in front of her as she watched the elves running around handing gifts to shoppers in the mall shopping.

Josephine stood with a sneer on her face showing her aggravation and waited for her turn to go see Santa. As the line grew behind them, all the sounds of excited kids seemed to blare at her. She could almost feel anger rising in her blood for her mother bringing her here.

Josephine watched as her mother waited at the exit, which Josephine couldn't wait to get to. She couldn't believe her mother was waiting for her so she could take a picture of her with a stranger of all things.

Her mom always told her, "Josephine, don't talk to strangers."

But now she has to sit on the lap of someone who couldn't be more of a stranger.

Ha, I'll get her, Josephine thought.

When she gets up to the fat man's lap, she's going to zip it and not say a word, and she's throwing away the key. With any luck, maybe the key will hit her mother's camera when she throws it.

Josephine watched as an elf at the top of the stairs grabbed the clip that held the handrail that kept the children at bay. She watched

Martha, who looked like she had two thousand ants up her dress, waited with glee for the man to welcome her up to make her dreams come true.

Josephine just wanted to do what Johnny does and barf right there. She waited and watched Martha as her pigtails swung back and forth with her glee as she ran up the stairs.

Josephine reached out and grabbed the short hairs at the top of her neck and yanked on them, causing Martha to scream out and turn around at her.

"Stop it," Martha yelled out at her as she turned around and gave her a dirty look.

Just then, an elf ran up to Josephine and put a piece of chocolate into her palm. Josephine looked down at the piece of chocolate and saw Santa winking at her.

Josephine looked over at Timmy, who was glaring at her because she had a beautiful piece of chocolate and he wanted it.

Maybe she would even give it to him if he asked her nicely enough. But no, Josephine looked at him and threw the piece of chocolate on the ground and stomped on it.

Timmy's hopes were dashed as he and Josephine looked down at the same time to see a completely smashed piece of chocolate looking back up at them. Santa was smashed. Brown chunks billowing out the cracks.

Just then, another elf ran up to them and placed a piece of chocolate into Timmy's hand, and with his excitement, he began tearing the wrapper off the piece of chocolate, and he dropped the wrapper on the floor.

My mother is going to be upset with me for doing that, he thought.

While he was thinking of his mother, the chocolate was snatched out of his hand. Timmy looked up only to see Josephine put the whole piece in her mouth.

"That one's yours," Josephine said to Timmy as she pointed down at the crumbled piece of chocolate on the floor as she began chewing. Then she smiled at him.

Josephine turned around and began watching as an elf at the top of the stairs pulled back the handrail and ran down the stairs and took Martha's hand. Then he escorted her up the stairs to where Santa held out his hand to her.

Josephine looked for the exit as Martha sat up and talked to him. She was going to go up there, and then she was going to run for the exit. If her mom wants to take a picture, then too bad!

She watched as Martha got up from the man's lap and was escorted by an elf to the exit. Then an elf ran down the stairs and grabbed her hand.

As she made it to the top of the steps, Santa reached out and took her hand and welcomed her to his knee, where he pulled her up and sat her down. She looked at Santa, and then she looked over at her mother as she snapped a picture of her.

"Hello, Josephine!" Santa said to her as he looked at her name tag.

"Hello, Santa," Josephine said to him as he looked at her with a lazy stare. His lazy stare made her want to have a nap right there.

"What would you like this year for Christmas, Josephine?" Santa said to her as he began to yawn.

Josephine's mind went blank, and she could feel the anger in her start to build for her mom bringing her here. She did not want to be here, and now she had no idea what to ask for.

Oh, my bageezers! she thought. She looked down at the exit where her mother stood looking proud and taking pictures of her as she watched.

"I want my mom to go fly a kite!" she yelled out at Santa and got up from his lap and ran for the exit.

Chapter

16

Timmy was excited when his mother woke him up early to get ready to go see Santa. She had made him some toast with sugar and cinnamon all over it and a bowl of oatmeal with a big glob of butter in it, just the way he liked it.

Timmy's only problem was that he was afraid. He was afraid of all the people and of the big man himself. He was going to feel like an elf when he sat on Santa's lap, and he was not going to pee. He was going to hold it! If he had to go, he would put his fingers in his ears to keep it from coming out either place.

He was excited to go to the Christmas Wonderland, and when they got to the mall, Timmy was so happy because he got to stand in line behind Martha and Josephine. He just hoped Johnny didn't get in line behind him because he would be a turd sandwich stuck between Johnny and Josephine.

There he stood behind Josephine in line. Timmy was amazed at all the things to watch and see. He was amazed at all the beautiful snow covered everything. The thousands of lights that glittered off the ceiling above. It was magical as he watched.

He was still mad at Josephine, who was standing in front of him getting yelled at by Martha. When he heard about a woman getting her leg ripped off, he stopped watching the elves and began watching Martha yelling at Josephine. He started to feel sorry for Josephine for getting yelled at by Martha, but after he heard about all the doll's body parts missing, he started to understand.

He can't remember how many times Josephine threw him off the pirate ship. She liked to give the old face-first treatment to an unsuspecting pirate with no sword. If you didn't have a sword, then it was overboard for you when she was around.

"I can't believe there isn't anybody here to see Santa," Timmy said to Johnny, who began standing in line behind him to his dismay. It then made sense to him. He was now a turd-faced sandwich. He had a turd face in front of him and a turd face behind him. They were going to ruin it for him for sure, he just knew it.

His excitement standing in line was only matched by the awe he saw in front of him as Santa sat in his chair and waved. The red was red and the black was black and the white made it all stand out. It was amazing.

It was the only time he had ever seen a Santa that wasn't ringing a bell.

The elves must have thrown all those other Santas out of the North Pole because they couldn't hand out presents right. Now they have to ring bells to say they're sorry, Timmy thought as he watched with excitement.

Santa was way bigger than he ever expected. He wasn't sure if his mom was going to be able to get a picture of him because he might disappear behind his belly. But he looked like a Santa that meant business. This was probably the kind of Santa who would bring you presents. He has seen other Santas that looked thin, but he knew they weren't the real Santa because the real Santa is fat.

Timmy watched as Santa sat down and the elves danced all about. Their glee was only matched by Martha waiting to be escorted to see him. He tried to watch around Josephine's shoulder, but she kept getting in his way on purpose so that he couldn't see.

Johnny, behind him, used him as a post to get higher to watch Martha as she climbed the stairs.

All that Timmy got to see was Martha as she ran down the stairs with a big smile on her face to where her mother took her in her arms and showed her the square picture that came out of the front of her camera. Martha was glowing as Timmy watched.

Then one of the elves came down and got Josephine and took her up to Santa, but Josephine sat on his lap for just a few seconds and got up and stomped down the stairs and through the gate where her mother stood. He watched as she walked past her mother and down the walkway out of sight.

Timmy was next in line, and an elf was coming down the stairs and grabbed his hand. Timmy instantly got scared. As the elf escorted him up the stairs to Santa. Santa grabbed him and pulled him down on his knee. Then Santa looked down at his name.

"Hello, Timmy," the Santa with the biggest facial hair he had ever seen said to him.

"Hello, Santa," Timmy replied, but he could barely get the words out.

"What would you like from Santa this year, Timmy?" Santa said to him as Timmy began to cower on his lap. He sat and looked up at Santa but his lips were frozen shut.

I don't want to pee out my ears! Timmy thought as he looked up into Santa's magical eyes. He was suddenly at a complete loss of what to say, and he couldn't remember what he wanted to ask for.

Timmy looked down at Johnny, and he was giving him the wedgie motion as he stood at the bottom of the stairs looking up at him and smiling. Then all Timmy could think about was the underwear stretching his butt crack.

Timmy reached his head forward and whispered into Santa's ear so he was sure that nobody else could hear. But all the noise that was going on around him made that impossible.

Timmy's mom took a picture of him talking with Santa and then he jumped off Santa's lap and began running down the exit ramp, pulling on his underwear as he went.

Chapter 17

"Mom, I can't sit on that man's lap. He is going to stink!" Johnny said to his mother as she drove straight ahead, singing along with Christmas songs, as they came and went on the radio.

Every time he sees a Santa that's ringing a bell, they all smell like they have been working all day, Johnny thought as he cringed at his mother as she sang along to Christmas songs.

"Santa is stupid!" Johnny kept saying to himself under his breath.

"Johnny, I want you to let me take a picture of you with Santa. Do you understand me?"

He pretended he didn't hear her and crossed his arms across his chest and stayed that way the whole time they drove to the mall. On a few occasions on their way, Johnny could feel a redness of anger arriving on his cheeks.

When they arrived at the mall, his mother pulled him over to the line where he saw Martha, Josephine, and Timmy standing in line—all waiting patiently to see Santa.

Johnny was happy to get into the line and at least get away from his mother because she was beginning to make him angry, but he didn't want to throw a fit in front of all the elves. It seemed to Johnny that they were acting bad enough on their own and wouldn't need any help from him.

Johnny walked down the line where Timmy was standing, and he wanted to be behind Martha, but every time he tried taking cuts in front of Timmy, he kept pushing him back. A little elf ran up to Johnny and handed him a little bar of chocolate, and he held it in his hand as the little long-eared fellow ran away.

A minute later, he took the piece of chocolate in his hand and threw it at Martha. It hit her in the back of the head. He saw as Martha turned around and smacked Josephine and told her to stop hitting her.

Johnny kept looking over at his mother. She was smiling, and she was so happy seeing her boy in line to go see Santa, but all Johnny wanted to do was kick Santa for being here and making him sit on his lap. Johnny wasn't going to do anything his mother asked him to do for at least a week for making him be here.

Timmy was looking around and watching all the elves that were running around, and Johnny kept trying to nudge his way in front of Timmy. He kept trying to block him with his body, but one block was too much for Johnny.

When Timmy turned around and began watching Martha as she went up the stairs, Johnny reached into the back of his pants and yanked upward on Timmy's underwear, giving him a huge wedgie. Timmy turned around and punched Johnny, but he knew it wouldn't do any good against him.

Timmy turned around and tried to ignore Johnny as he tried pulling his underwear down out of his crack.

Both of them watched as Martha and then Josephine was escorted up to the fat man sitting and waiting for them. After Josephine got up and ran for the exit, that was when Johnny made his move and slammed Timmy behind him, making Johnny next in line. Johnny wanted to go see Santa and make his way to the exit so he could go home and pick on kids the rest of the day.

Standing in front of Timmy and trying to keep him from cutting front of him came to an end when an elf came down and grabbed Timmy's hand and escorted him up to see Santa.

"I didn't want to go next anyway," Johnny declared as the elf escorted Timmy up the stairs.

After Timmy ran for the exit, Johnny felt his hand grabbed by one of the elves, and Johnny looked up to see Santa glaring down at him.

Then Johnny looked over at his mother, and she had the biggest smile on her face. All the blood in Johnny's body raced for his face.

When he got to the top of the steps, Santa reached out and grabbed his hand and gave a yank on Johnny and pulled him up onto his knee. Johnny looked into Santa's eyes, and they were cold when they looked back at him.

At that moment he wanted to turn around and make his way to the exit, but his mom wanted a picture, so he would give her two seconds to get one before he jumped from Santa's lap.

"Hello, Johnny," Santa said as he looked down at his name tag. His deep voice silenced Johnny as he stared up at him.

"Hello, Santa," Johnny said back to him with no interest in saying another word to him.

"And what would you like from Santa this year, Johnny?" Santa said to him as he glared back at him.

Johnny looked over to where his mother was trying to take a picture. She made him so mad he could just burst. Then Johnny looked up at Santa.

"I want a new mom!" Johnny said to Santa as he glared down at him. Then Johnny jumped up off his lap and ran to the exit where his mom stood looking furious at him.

Chapter

18

For days Martha was excited that she got to see Santa and couldn't wait for him to come down the chimney. She could still remember looking up at him and seeing him wink at her before lifting her from his knee.

She could still see the snow globe with a man and woman skating in it clearly in her mind.

Sitting on the real Santa's lap was something that hardly any kid ever gets to do, she thought.

And almost all of his elves were there too! But there were probably a million more up North, she figured. He couldn't deliver all those presents with just four elves, could he?

Martha walked out into her backyard, where the sun began warming her face. She was sad there wasn't going to be a white Christmas, but she was happy she was going to get to draw in the dirt after the sun had melted all the snow and dried out their dirt patch.

The children of the neighborhood were abandoning calls for silence and retorting with loud gestures of play and the occasional sound of a scream perpetuated by an elbow wound.

Martha found herself a stick and went to the back patch of dirt where she liked to draw. She sat down in her nice dress and shoes. She told her mom that she had to wear her dress and shoes until Santa got here because he wouldn't know it was her if she didn't.

Martha's mom let her fulfill her wishes by keeping them for three days in a row. It would be sad when on day four her mother said, "At least let me wash them for you, and you can put your Santa dress and socks back on."

As Martha sat in the dirt and drew butterflies, Josephine walked down the street out front and saw her in the backyard sitting. Josephine stopped walking and came into the backyard and found a stick and sat down next to Martha to draw with her.

Silently, the two of them drew figures in the sand. It was a silent hello they had both shared.

"Why do you always draw butterflies?" Josephine asked Martha as she began to draw.

"Because one day I will have wind beneath my wings," Martha said to her with a dreamy look on her face.

Johnny walked into the backyard and saw the two of them and began looking for a stick to dig in the sand with before he came over and sat across from them.

Johnny began digging with his stick in the dirt. Johnny always liked to dig holes in the dirt patch. Martha wasn't sure if he was ever going to stop digging sometimes.

"Johnny, you're going to find a rabbit's foot if you dig any deeper!" Josephine said as she looked over at him and watched him dig furiously with his stick into the hard ground.

"My butt crack itches something fierce," Josephine said as she reached around and started scratching it.

"Josephine? Did Martha come over to your house?" Johnny said as he continued digging a hole for himself.

Martha stopped drawing with her stick and stayed frozen in place as she looked down.

"Yeah, I think so. Last night she did, sure. Why?" Josephine said as she looked up at Johnny.

"No reason," Johnny said as he continued to look down as he dug.

Martha felt relieved as she looked down and started drawing again. She didn't want to look up because if she did, she might start laughing so hard she would surely pee.

Hello Santa

Timmy came into the yard carrying his dump truck and sat down next to Johnny and began moving the truck back and forth, breaking up the dirt.

"Hi, Timmy," Martha said as she stopped drawing to watch him. "You know," Martha began as she started to draw birds in the sand. "We might not always get along, but we should always be friends forever—even if Josephine is a jerk."

The four of them stopped what they were doing and looked at each other.

Josephine looked at Martha through her long, straight black hair that was hanging in her face, making her look like a ghoul, and stuck her tongue out at her and then smiled.

"Johnny might be a real jerk sometimes," Timmy began as he loaded his dump truck with dirt. "But remember that day when Marty pushed Josephine down and started hitting her? Johnny hit him and then shoved a goose turd in his mouth!"

They all began to laugh as they thought of it.

"But now Josephine calls everybody turd face instead of just him," Martha said as she erased her birds and started drawing Miss Barb with her arm back.

"Every time I wear these underwear, my butt itches," Johnny said as he began itching his butt.

The four of them continued playing and drawing in the dirt together until Martha broke the silence.

"Timmy, what did you ask Santa for Christmas?" she asked him as she continued drawing.

"I don't remember," he said as he began filling his dump truck so full of sand that it began spilling over.

"I asked for a new bike, and I better get one because if I don't, then I'm not ever going to see Santa again!" Johnny said as he looked at Martha and waited for a reply.

"I asked Santa to make me famous for Christmas," Josephine said as everybody stopped what they were doing and looked at her.

"I have to go poop!" Timmy said as he jumped up and started running toward his house down the street.

"Josephine, you can't ask Santa to do something for you! You have to get something from him, dummy!" Johnny said as he looked across at her.

"Yes, I can! I can ask Santa for anything. You're a boy, Johnny Ingersol, and boys don't know anything! Just ask Martha. She is the smartest kid in school!"

Johnny looked over at Martha.

"It's true," Martha said as she continued to draw in the sand. "I'm the smartest girl in school, Johnny Ingersol, and I hereby proclaim you are stupid!"

Johnny glared over at Martha, who now had a dark circle around her lips after grabbing Timmy's juice bottle. Then she handed it to Josephine, and after they drank, they both looked down and continued to play in the dirt, knowing that they had both broken Timmy's rule of not drinking from his juice bottle.

It is a beautiful day out, Johnny thought as he thought about Timmy's absence for far longer than he thought he would be gone.

Johnny got up and picked up Timmy's dump truck and began to walk away to the side of the house with it.

Martha and Josephine watched as he went around the corner and came back a minute later, careful not to spill the contents of Timmy's dump truck. Johnny came back and sat down.

"Santa is real, and you have to ask for a toy because that's all Santa can give you because that's the only thing the elves know how to make," Martha said as Timmy came back panting and sat down after running from his house.

"Santa is stupid!" Johnny said as he watched Timmy start to scoop the wet sand out of the back of his dump truck. Timmy looked over at his juice bottle and saw that it was empty.

"Why did you pour my juice into my dump truck? Johnny, you're stupid!" Timmy said as he began scooping the wet sand out of it.

Martha and Josephine both looked away as Timmy looked over at them and got suspicious.

"Johnny peed in it, Timmy," Josephine said as Timmy stopped digging the wet sand out.

He looked at the juice bottle and then up at Johnny. He had a laughter caught in his gut that was about to explode, and Timmy wondered with all his might whether something other than laughter was going to come out with it.

Then he looked over at Josephine and Martha, and both of them were staring at him, each one of them had a dark circle around their lips.

Chapter

19

It was like Martha had ants in her pants all night long. She knew that Santa was never going to come if she didn't go to sleep, so she slammed her eyes shut and held them shut because if she made her eyeballs tired they would have to go to sleep.

The next morning she was so happy to hear her mother calling her downstairs and telling her Merry Christmas from the bottom of the stairs.

Martha threw off her covers and put on her slippers and went running down the stairs. She was going so fast she had to hang on to the railing to keep her from falling backward because her feet were going so fast.

When she got downstairs, she went into the living room where her mother sat next to the tree. She went and sat down next to her mother by the tree, and she said, "I love you, Momma. Merry Christmas," and she hugged her mother tight.

Her mother grabbed a present out from under the tree and handed it to her. Martha opened the present, and when she saw it, her heart almost leaped out of her chest.

It was the most beautiful doll she had ever seen. She was in awe of the beauty.

"Oh, thank you, Momma!" Martha said as she gave her a great big hug.

Martha's mother handed her presents, and Martha was so happy Santa came to see them. Martha got all the socks a girl could ask for, but it was enough for her. Her doll was the most beautiful she had ever seen.

Martha turned to watch her mother as she opened a card that somebody had given her. Martha stared at her doll and watched her mother as her mother pulled out a ticket from her card.

"I'm sorry I didn't get you a present, Momma," Martha told her mother as she began to watch her scratching at the little ticket.

Suddenly, as Martha stared into her doll's beautiful eyes, her mother began to scream and howl that almost frightened Martha half to death.

"We're rich, Martha!" her mother began screaming.

Martha looked at her mother and smiled, but she didn't understand what her momma meant. She did know she had never seen her mother so happy. Martha now understood how people could cry when they're happy.

When her mom explained to her about everything, then she understood and was so happy that she cried with happiness for the first time in her life.

Martha looked out the window and said, "Thank you, Santa!" Believing that no matter what direction she looked, the North Pole would always be in that direction.

Martha began watching her momma as she sat on the couch and continued to cry with all her excited happiness.

"Momma, it's a wonderful day," Martha said as she rubbed one of the happy tears out of the corner of her mother's eye. "Momma, I am going to march upstairs and get Miss Molly, and we can all celebrate such a wonderful Christmas by having some humble pie together!"

Martha turned around and began marching toward the stairs. She was so excited to show Miss Molly all her new presents.

"Martha dear, please come over and sit with me. I think I've had all the humble pie I could stand."

Chapter 20

Timmy woke up, and it was Christmas morning, and the sun was shining bright into his window. He lay in his bed listening to see if his mother was up yet. She was woken up by him almost every morning, so on Christmas morning, he was sure to be the only one up and about.

As he looked out his window, he was so glad it was going to be warm out so he could take his presents outside to show them to his friends—when he found out what they were.

Timmy was excited about Christmas morning, but he couldn't remember what he asked for from Santa. He tried and tried to remember, but he knew that when he opened his present from Santa, it would be what he asked for.

His mom was sure to always get him good presents, and Santa always brought him something he couldn't even remember asking for. He liked making presents for his mother, and this year he made her a card and a present so she would have lots of presents to open too.

Timmy got up and marched downstairs, hoping to wake his mother if she wasn't already up. When he came downstairs, his mother was sitting on the couch and drinking her coffee before she had to clean up after him all day.

The first thing he saw when he looked at the tree was a new bike sitting behind it. Timmy began to scream with joy, but then he stopped himself. He was going to save all that noise to share with Johnny when he showed Johnny his new, beautiful white bike.

Timmy knew that Johnny was going to get a new bike for Christmas, so Timmy was glad that they would now both have two brand-new bikes to ride together side by side. Johnny was going to be so happy to see that he got a new bike too. He might even be able to beat Johnny in a race around the block.

Timmy finished opening all his presents, and he was happy. He sat on the couch with his mother, careful not to spill her coffee. She would get him a good one if he did. She might even become a pirate mom. And Timmy could never sword fight his mother.

"Timmy?" his mother said to him as he stared down at all his presents. He still doesn't remember what he asked Santa for, but he was sure he would get an answer if he tapped his forehead four hundred times like Martha said to do.

"Timmy, I have another gift for you."

Timmy looked up at her with wonderment on his face.

"Timmy, your father is coming home, and he will never leave us again."

Timmy just stared at his mother, and a tear gathered in the corner of his eye.

Chapter

21

"Josephine!" she heard her mother call out. She opened her eyes and looked up and couldn't believe it. Why did she have to wake her up? She was sleeping as pleasant as a winter day with lots of snow, and her mother ruined it. Her mother was so annoying.

Josephine didn't know how many times she had told her mother that she didn't want to be disturbed, and her mother never listened to her. She just wanted to lie here all day and not be bothered with Christmas. Was that too much to ask for?

"Josephine?" her mother yelled up to her again. "Please come down here."

It was Christmas morning, and her mother was always excited about the morning of Christmas.

As far back as she could remember, her mom made a big fuss all day. She would want to open presents and play with all her toys. She couldn't remember what she asked for from Santa, but she wanted to go back to bed anyway.

Josephine would leave little notes around the house for her mother to find, and on these little notes were written little messages. *"I want a guitar for Christmas"* or *"I want a chalk set."* She didn't want to make it easy for her mother.

The first thing her mother made her do Christmas morning was to open all her presents. Her mother would take pictures, but Josephine always used her hair to cover her face, and her mom always fussed at her to move it out of her eyes.

Then it was breakfast, then off into the car, where they drove around all day going to people's houses to visit and give them stuff. She even had to carry everything.

Who would ever want to get out of bed in the morning and then go driving around all day giving people presents? she wondered.

Her mother was a busybody, and she could never figure out why her mother did the things she does. Why would someone do stuff just to do stuff? Why would they spend so much time making things pretty just to make them not pretty again?

Her mom liked making the house look pretty, but anything that was pretty was not for Josephine. She wanted it the way it was. All that work. Not her.

"Josephine! Hurry up!" her mother screamed up at her as she threw off her covers.

"Ugh," Josephine said as she went over to her door.

"I don't want any presents!" she screamed out her door as she slammed it closed. She turned around and got her slippers on and prepared herself for another Christmas day with her mother.

Josephine made her way down the stairs, and as she went downstairs, she noticed that all the windows were open and that her mother was outside sitting in the sun and having a cup of coffee.

"Mother! I'm ready to open all of my presents!" Josephine called out as she sat down at the tree to open her presents.

"Merry Christmas, Josephine!" her mother said to her as she came into the room and sat down beside her to watch her open her presents.

Josephine began opening the presents as fast as her mother could hand them to her, but there wasn't one present that she liked so far. All of the presents were socks, dresses, and shoes.

"Where are my good presents!" Josephine said to her mother with an angry tone in her voice.

Her mother reached under the tree and pulled out a long box and handed it to her.

"Here I got something for you that we can both enjoy together," her mother said to her as Josephine snatched the gift out of her hand.

Furiously, she ripped off the paper to see what was waiting inside the box for her.

"What is it?" she asked her mother as she fought with the box to get it open. Josephine wanted to throw it at that very moment. It was just a trick that her mother was playing on her. Like birthday candles that keep relighting.

"Open the box, dear."

Josephine yanked the box open that still had pieces of tape holding it closed. She finally got it open and then looked inside, and her jaw almost bounced off the floor. She had absolutely no words to describe what she was thinking.

"It's a dozen kites for you to play with this summer. I know how you love flying kites."

Her mother grabbed the box from her and set it down on the floor and grabbed a kite out of the box.

"Come on, Josephine. I want to go fly a kite! It's a beautiful day, Josephine!"

Josephine looked up at her mother in despair. All she could hear herself saying was, "Santa!"

Chapter 22

Johnny wasn't excited about Christmas like the other kids were, but he still liked presents. Who wouldn't want free stuff, especially when all you have to do is ask for it? Christmas should be every day so that every day he could ask for something and get it.

When he woke up the only thing, the first thing that came to his mind was how wonderful his new bike was going to be. It's going to be white like a cloud and faster than a bolt of lightning! At least, that's what he was hoping.

Johnny woke up and just wanted to lie there. He had to talk himself into getting up before he was going to go downstairs. He was still sore from falling on his face when he tried riding his bike in the snow.

His mother was never up on Christmas morning, and she always made him wait until she got up so she could watch him open his presents. Then she wanted to take a bunch of stupid pictures of him holding them.

This year Johnny was not going to wait for his mother to wake up for him to open his presents. He was going to go down there and open them because he didn't want her taking pictures anyway.

His mom always asked him to do things around the house, but he never did any of it. She never found out he didn't do his chores because he has never once gotten coal on Christmas. Johnny has a feeling that maybe he might not be the greatest son to his mother. But it's Christmas morning, and no kid should be bothered with such things on Christmas!

Johnny got up out of bed and put on his slippers. He made his way out of his bedroom door and creeped out of his room toward the stairs. The floor squeaked as he stepped, so he stopped. He wanted to make sure that his mother couldn't hear him.

He moved as quietly as he could and when he got down to the bottom of the stairs he looked into the living room, and Johnny had never seen so many presents in his life.

He wanted to be as quiet as he could be, but when he saw all the presents, he lost his mind. He ran down the stairs, not caring if he made noise or not, and went to his knees and slid across the floor on his pajamas and stopped sliding in front of the tree. He grabbed the first present he saw and opened it.

"Wow, a remote-controlled airplane!" he said as he threw it down on the floor and grabbed another present and opened it.

"Wow, a brand-new baseball mitt!" he said as he threw it down and grabbed and opened presents one after the other.

He had hit the jackpot, and he couldn't believe it. He thought but couldn't remember what he asked Santa for, but he was sure it was one of these things.

"Maybe going to see Santa does work!" Johnny said as he kept grabbing presents and opening them.

Behind him, the kitchen door swung open, and his mom gasped as she walked into the room behind him. Then Johnny looked up at his mom, and he gasped.

His mother was all made up with makeup, and her hair was a different color, and it was long and blond with beautiful curls. Her long dress made her look like a movie star. This couldn't possibly be his mom! His mom didn't care if he did what he wanted to do!

"What have you done, Johnny Ingersol?" his mother said to him as she looked down at the mess that was spread everywhere in the living room. "Those weren't your presents!" she screamed at him in horror. "Those were for your nieces and nephews. Your present is over there!" She pointed to a bike in the corner.

And boy, did it deserve to look lonely. It was pink, and it was nothing like what he had longed for. The long yellow banana seat looked like it had carried many butt cracks all over town if he guessed it.

"That can't be my bike! It's a girl's bike!" Johnny said as he looked up into his mother's flowing curls as she leaned back and stood fully upright glaring down at him.

"I found it! It was free."

Johnny stood there looking at her in complete and utter shock.

"Johnny Ingersol, you will rewrap all those present this instant!" his mother declared a matter- of-factly to him.

"Shuuut! Uuuup!" Johnny shouted at the top of his voice at his now movie-star-looking mother standing only three feet away from him.

That was the instant he saw it, and it was like one of those big bumblebees that appear in the corner of your eye. Only this bee sting was going to be of the five-finger variety.

Then her slap arrived on his left cheek, which had been sitting there waiting for her to set upon it. Then he saw an instantaneous explosion of light as if it were coming to life on the Fourth of July.

His mother had officially declared a five-finger discipline down payment on his cheek with a quite impressive investment.

Johnny stood stunned as his mother looked down at him. He was stunned and amazed all at the same time. Is that what he needed? Johnny had an instantaneous thought that arrived in his head, and then his mother spoke.

"I want to be a new mom! I want to raise you right. With discipline and with love. I am tired of you being disrespectful to your elders. That means anybody older than you. And you should look after the younger kids! And your friends!"

Johnny was almost going to fall over, but there was only one thing that he could think about— Santa!

Chapter 23

It was such a beautiful day for Martha. She had gotten everything she had ever wanted and will want for Christmas. But Martha knew that if there was ever anything important that she needed to ask Santa for, then she was going to save her biggest ask for Santa and everything else for her mother.

She walked out the back door in her dress and shoes, and she never wanted to take them off. Now her dress and her shoes were good luck, she couldn't take them off! Maybe in a couple of days, Martha thought, her mother could wash them.

Martha was so happy that she got to see her mother cry because she was happy. She could never have believed such a thing had she not seen it with her own two eyes.

Martha is excited about going away. She is going to miss her friends though. Her mother told her that she isn't moving away far enough that she couldn't still see them now and again, but Martha had to move closer to the new school that she was going to go to.

Martha was so excited about going to a secret school. She guessed that maybe only important kids went there if it was a secret school. After all, spies go to school there. That's what Josephine thinks, and Martha believes her.

She will miss Josephine. Timmy calls her mean, but she doesn't think that Josephine is mean. She just thinks that Josephine speaks in different ways. Maybe she is mean to Timmy because she likes him. She didn't know. She knew that she would miss playing with her friends, drawing in the dirt with them. Most of all, she thinks about going to see Santa with them.

—m—

Martha looks back on it now and thinks maybe the reason she loved that memory of going to see Santa so much was because she was there with her friends.

Thirty years later, Martha is practicing law, but she made up her mind not to be the lying kind. That is, if she can help it. She services people who need protection from the same kind of scrooges that would break into a kids' house and steal all their presents, but the scrooges she fights usually have a lot of money and try to steal everyone's presents.

Martha remembers her childhood and has such wonderful memories with her friends; and because of them, every year, she makes sure she goes to see Santa.

Chapter 24

It was the last day of their Christmas vacation, and it was the only day that Johnny would be able to play outside. Johnny was walking in front of Martha's house when he saw her in the backyard with her beautiful dress on and her white socks and black shoes.

He knew that she loved that outfit. She didn't mind getting dirty, but he knew that when she had that outfit on, she would try to stay as clean as she could.

Johnny stopped walking and watched her from the street as she drew in the dirt. He walked up the driveway, and when he got to the edge of the house, he stood there and watched her. She kept throwing her pigtails behind her every time they fell back into her face.

Johnny came around the house and walked in the yard and began looking for a stick. She looked up and saw him walking toward her, and she looked back down and continued to draw.

He sat down a couple of feet from her and began drawing in the dirt with her.

"My mom says I'm going to a secret school, so I can't talk about it," Martha said as she drew in the dirt.

"It's not a secret school, it's a private school, silly. Where girls wear pretty dresses and boys get told what to do all the time. I wouldn't want to go there because I would have a sore foot from all the shin kicking I would have to do," Johnny said as he began digging a hole.

How deep? He wasn't sure yet.

"My mom grounded me for three months. She said I had to pay for my past misdeeds. I told her that I would pay for it with my allowance, but she said it wasn't painful enough. Three months in my room is more like torture!" Johnny said.

Martha laughed, and he began to giggle with her.

"Martha?" Johnny said to her in a soft voice.

"What, Johnny?" Martha was still mad at him for sending her into the creek, but she did like to have someone to draw with. She looked over and saw that he had drawn a picture of a girl and a boy holding hands.

"Martha?" he said as she looked up at him. "I just wanted to tell you that I'm sorry for pushing you into the creek."

He began drawing an umbrella in the boy figure's hand that was holding the umbrella over the girl's stick figure head. Then he began to draw raindrops.

"Do you know why I pushed you into the creek, Martha?" Johnny said as he stopped drawing and looked up at her. "Because I don't want anyone else doing it but me. Maybe you want to make it to the creek. And if you do want to make it down to the creek, then I will help you. You might not like getting wet when you do, but maybe you like being the only one that can make it to the creek. With my help, of course!" Johnny said with pride. "That's love, Martha." Johnny started to dig another hole for himself.

Martha looked up at Johnny with wonderment in her eyes.

"I guess," Martha said and looked down and began sticking her stick into the dirt. Then she started moving dirt around, being careful not to get any on her dress.

"You know why I pick on other kids, Martha? I don't like picking on kids, but if I pick on them, then they won't pick on me." Johnny looked down and began digging his hole deeper. "My butt crack itches something fierce," Johnny said as he reached behind him to start digging.

But instead of inserting his hand in his crack, Johnny reached out and grabbed Martha's nipple and squeezed and twisted it as hard and as fast as he could.

Martha's wrath was going to be epic, and he was expecting it, but he never expected to have an everyday reminder from that day at the dirt pit in Martha's backyard.

"Titty twister!" Johnny screamed as he squeezed as hard as he could and rose to his feet in the same motion. As soon as he made it to his feet, he turned around and began running as Martha howled from the sting.

Without even thinking about it, Martha drew her hand back, and in a steady and swift motion, she pulled her arm back and let her reaction aim. She threw her stick at Johnny as hard as she could, and to her amazement, her stick hit Johnny in the back of his ear and went right through it.

It stung as all get out as he started to run away from the dirt pit, away from Martha and away from some of the best times he had ever had in his life.

He loved Martha, but that was for the twister she gave him in the hall on their last day of school before Christmas vacation.

As Johnny was walking down the hall, calling Timmy Pickle Crack, Martha walked by him and gave him a ten-finger titty twister. She used two hands to grab and twist. It hurt so bad, and he was chaffed for two days. He promised her he would get her back.

Johnny didn't see Martha for a long time after that. She moved away, and he never got to say goodbye. Other than that day in the dirt. But every night, Johnny looks up into the sky when the stars are shining bright and gleaming with light that had been sent to his sight long ago and says, "I love you, Martha Morris."

Thirty years later, Johnny is still selling cars, and he still has the scar on the back of his ear where Martha threw a stick through it. He remembered all the early days and all the fun they used to have. Well, Johnny remembered it as fun. Everybody else might remember it as torture.

He still remembered the day that Martha had sent him on his life's path of the future.

Martha looked at him one day and said, "You'll probably sell cars when you grow up because my mom says that those people lie to people for a living! And, Johnny Ingersol, when you open your word hole, the lying ones always come out!"

He always listened to Martha, whether she believed it or not. And every year, he always goes to see Santa.

Chapter

25

Martha got up and had to go get a new stick because hers was now sticking out of Johnny's ear as he ran down the street, howling.

She found a new stick and sat down, and she erased her drawing by smoothing out the dirt with her hand and began drawing snow angels on the sand with her fingers, sliding them gently back and forth in the sand.

Martha sat drawing in the sand, and after, she would make an angel masterpiece. She was going to make one that was just butterflies on a flower.

She was glad that it was the last day of the Christmas vacation. She got everything she wanted from Santa, and seeing her mom as happy as she was, was more than worth her first in-person ask from Santa himself. Now she knew for sure that he was the real Santa.

She began to hear footsteps behind her, and she turned around to look over to see Josephine dredging through the yard, looking for a good stick to draw in the dirt with.

"What are you going to draw?" she asked her as she picked up a stick and walked over to where she was sitting and sat down next to her. Both of them had a light trace of the ink that made a circle around their lips.

"Hello, Martha," she said as she began drawing in the dirt. "I think I'm going to draw animals today. If we are going to eat them, then at least we can do is draw pictures of them. I like animals and usually, people draw what they like."

The two of them continued to draw as they always did. Most often Martha lost all contests with Josephine. Hers was always nicer or prettier. Martha didn't mind though. Josephine would always be her friend no matter how wrong she was.

Josephine got up from her spot at the edge of the dirt patch. She walked to Martha and stood looking down at her until Martha looked up at her.

"Good luck, turd face!" Josephine said as she held her black hair back with one hand and leaned over to Martha and kissed her on the forehead.

Martha looked up at Josephine before she turned away, and tears had begun to run down her cheek.

Josephine walked down the driveway and turned in the direction of home. She looked at the trees with the bright colors all lit up inside the homes as she passed them. She would let the tears of friendship flow for as long as they wished. Then she heard it.

"I love you, turd face!" she heard Martha scream at the top of her voice from the dirt pit.

Josephine stopped, and she looked up from the sidewalk and looked back toward Martha's house. A small smile began to form on her lips.

"I love you too, Martha Morris!" Josephine screamed out as loud as she could.

Thirty years later, Josephine sat in the large dining room that was now empty of all patrons. She enjoyed playing in her band called *Turd Face*.

She thought of her friends often and the wonderful times she had as a child and all the times she has gone to see Santa. With Christmas arriving soon and quickly, as it most often did, she looks around at everything she has and she is grateful.

"All because of Santa," she said to herself as she looked around once more.

What was a small bar she had purchased at one time became a large bar, and then a restaurant with a bar. And then it became a hotel that had a restaurant and a bar and a place for her band to play.

But no matter how busy life gets and how hard it is to find time to do things, Josephine always finds time to go see Santa.

Chapter

26

Every morning after Christmas, the sun was out, and the birds seemed to be at their loudest. All the kids got to take out their new bikes and everyone got to have fun because Johnny was grounded to his room.

Day after day, Timmy would ride by Johnny's house on his new bike to show it off, and Johnny would be looking out the window at him steaming, thinking about the yellow banana seat downstairs in the corner. Johnny was trapped in a bedroom prison, and there was no way for him to get out of it.

Timmy missed his friend Johnny, but only a little bit. Now it was his turn to pay back for the pickle, so every day Timmy would drive his bike by Johnny's house so he could tease him on his new bike.

"*It's not pink!*" one of his notes read.

On his way over to Martha's, he decided to stop at Johnny's and show his note to him for today. Johnny looked down and threw his fist up at Timmy when he read it.

It said, "*See you at school!*"

After rapidly exiting Johnny's yard in fear of a chair coming out a window, Timmy rode his bike over to Martha's, where he found her drawing in the sand in her backyard at the dirt pit.

Timmy looked for a stick in the yard and sat down by Martha, and the two of them sat and drew in the sand.

"My mom says that I don't have to go to school anymore," Martha said as she outlined a butterfly in the dirt. "She said that I'm going to start going to a secret school, so I don't think I'm supposed to talk about it. I think it is supposed to be a secret. I think that's where I'm going, to a secret school."

Timmy looked at Martha and said, "We better not talk about it then."

The two of them sat and drew in the sand and talked about what they got for Christmas.

"Martha!" Timmy said as he got a big smile on his face and started laughing. "I remembered what I asked for from Santa!" Timmy said as he got up and started dancing around and screaming, "Thank you, Santa! Thank you, Santa!"

"Timothy Parker, stop your dancing right this minute!" Martha said. She wanted him to stop so he could tell her what he was talking about.

"You called me by my name, Martha!" Timmy said. It was the first time she had ever called him by his full name.

"I don't call you by your real name because your name makes you sound smart. So I can't call you by your real name. Timmy Parker,

Both of them began to laugh.

"Martha, I remembered what I asked for from Santa!"

"What did you ask for!" Martha asked as she pointed her stick at him.

"I asked Santa for Johnny to get what he deserves!" Timmy belted out in laughter.

—⚘—

Timmy always looks back and remembers his childhood fondly. He sat and thought about all the times he used to take his juice bottle with him.

Every time he left the house, no matter where he was going, he would always take his juice bottle. But before he left the house with it, he would go up to his room and put blue ink on the edge of the bottle very carefully. Then he would put the lid on.

He never actually drank from the juice bottle; but occasionally, as he played, he would see a kid run by with a circle around his lips from drinking from that juice container.

All the kids at the playground would end up with circles on their faces eventually, but Timmy always kept that a secret.

Thirty years later, Timmy is working as a dentist.

Johnny, the day he knocked out his tooth on Gobbler's Hill, showed Timmy his life's path. To make sure that everybody gets their tooth back to give to the tooth fairy—or replace it for a great deal of money! As for Santa? Timmy goes to see him every year.

Timmy sat in his dentist's chair and looked out the window and watched as the leaves that had changed color so vibrantly drifted slowly by on a gust of wind. Soon the smell of autumn would give way to Johnny Ingersol's favorite time of year—winter.

He reached over and picked up the phone and dialed it, and then the other end began to ring.

"Hello?" a voice said through the phone to him.

"Do you want to go see Santa with me this year?" Timmy said into the phone.

"Okay," Josephine said. "I'll see if Martha and Johnny want to go too."

"Okay, I love you, Josephine!" Timmy said.

"I love you too, turd face!"

The End

Next

Hello, Santa
Book Two
A Christmas Story Reunion

Disclaimer:

Anyone under the age of twenty-one may not understand the complexities of that story.

www.ingramcontent.com/pod-product-compliance
Lightning Source LLC
LaVergne TN
LVHW041455100625
813500LV00031B/238